DRAWING
SYBYLLA

ABOUT THE AUTHOR

Dr Odette Kelada is a Lecturer in Creative Writing in the School of Culture and Communication. She has a PhD in literature researching the lives of Australian women writers. Her writing focuses on marginalised voices, gender and racial literacy, and has appeared in numerous publications including the *Australian Cultural History Journal*, *Outskirts*, *Postcolonial Studies* and the *Journal of the Association for the Study of Australian Literature*.

DRAWING SYBYLLA

THE REAL AND IMAGINED LIVES OF AUSTRALIA'S WRITING WOMEN

ODETTE KELADA

UWA PUBLISHING

First published in 2017 by
UWA Publishing
Crawley, Western Australia 6009
www.uwap.uwa.edu.au

UWAP is an imprint of UWA Publishing,
a division of The University of Western Australia.

National Library of Australia Cataloguing-in-Publication data:
Kelada, Odette, author.
Drawing sybylla / Odette Kelada.
ISBN: 9781742589510 (paperback)
Creative writing—Fiction.
Women authors, Australian—21st century—Fiction.
Australian fiction.

Cover design by Alissa Dinallo
Typeset in 11 pt Bembo by Lasertype
Printed by Lightning Source

This project has been assisted by the Australian Government
through the Australia Council, its arts funding and advisory body.

This project is supported by the Copyright Agency Cultural Fund.

 uwapublishing

For my family –
for holding everything

'I am given to something which a man never pardons in a woman. You will draw away as though I were a snake when you hear it.' With this warning, Sybylla confesses to her rich and handsome suitor that she is given to writing stories and bound, therefore, on a brilliant career.

Publisher's endorsement for
Miles Franklin's *My Brilliant Career*,
Centenary Edition, 2001.

Contents

Scene from a Writers' Festival

Sybil was bred in a light cave. A light cave is one with a hole in the roof. Pronouncements from the gods descended through this celestial skylight, littering the floor with divine detritus. She scrawled holy words on leaves and bark. But they were never hers. They always came from beyond or below. For this cave marked the entrance to the Underworld. All that was past and buried would lick the undersides of the leaves as they fell from her hand. In Ancient Greece, 'The Sybils' were mad mouthpieces babbling unintelligible insights, writing illegible poetry.

The woman onstage is named Sybil. Sybil Jones. Her skin does not have the pallor of a cavern dweller, though something in her stature bears the breeding of an oracle. But her biographic notes say she was born in Albury-Wodonga, far from the cave at Cumae, a world away from Hecate's lake. I stare at her through the glass of water in front of me. Behind her head, the audience swims in rows of liquid faces. If humans are seventy per cent water, is a crowd an ocean? Is that what is meant by a sea of people?

I pick up my pen and dribble ink onto the page. Flowers grow either side of the red margin. Monstrous petals with goblin faces leer from the middle of them. At the lectern Sybil is speaking. I see the back of her hair from my position onstage. She looks like the stalk of one of my flowers, long body dripping into high, quirky heels – quirky as they are forties-style pumps, jarrah brown. With her chocolate stockings and long red skirt she is a warm wood fire. I can see her burning away in front of me, alight with passion for something. She catches me for a moment. Rare as it is at these events, I find myself listening.

'I think that woman goes out in the daytime! And I'll tell you why – privately – I've seen her! I can see her out of every one of my windows!'

Out of every one? How many windows does this person have? The rest of us have only one or two at the most and some people are totally boarded up, not a rasp of daylight in them.

'I see her on the long road under the trees, creeping along, and when the carriage comes she hides under the blackberry vines. I don't blame her a bit. It must be very humiliating to be caught creeping by daylight!'

Creeping by daylight. My goblins love this. They laugh and the ink on my paper stirs. I feel this. All the time. Every minute. Even here in front of this big crowd I am creeping, skulking behind the shadow of my persona: writer, charming, lady…I cannot peel my eyes from the chocolate fire as she reads, red lips round.

'And though I always see her, she may be able to creep faster than I can turn! I have watched her sometimes away off in the open country, creeping as fast as a cloud shadow in a wind.'

What was I just saying? Cloud shadows! This woman is reading my thoughts. It must be all her windows. Is that it? Is that how she can see everything? See into me? The volume Sybil is holding up is thick and old. There is dust in its pages. I can smell it! Most writers at these things read their own stuff. Isn't that the point? Why else would you bother to come? Perhaps she has gone off on a tangent. Perhaps she is referencing. Surely not one of the greats. No one references the greats when they're about to read their own work.

'*If only that top pattern could be gotten off from the under one! I mean to try it, little by little.*'

Patterns…The red skirt has patterns all up it. Swirls and vines. They could run all the way to her neck and make a necklace around the nape of brown skin. A blackberry vine to choke on. What does 'top pattern' mean anyway? And if there's a pattern under a pattern then wouldn't they all be one pattern? That's the point of patterns, isn't it? To fold under, interlace, come around…and all that. Sybil pauses. It is a dramatic pause, I think. Yes, she shuts the book with due gravitas.

'*The Yellow Wallpaper*,' she says, 'has inspired me to pursue many patterns. In my own life as well as on the page. Charlotte Perkins Gilman wrote this tale of claustrophobic confinement while confined herself to her sickbed. Except she wasn't sick. She had just given birth. We would call it postnatal depression and recommend fresh air, activity and a break from the stresses of motherhood. The rest cure prescribed to Charlotte by her doctor was, "Live as domestic a life as possible. Have your child with you all the time… Lie down an hour after each meal. Have but two hours' intellectual life a day. And never touch pen, brush or pencil as long as you live." From this madness comes *The Yellow Wallpaper*.'

Sybil turns and reaches for her water on the table. Her hand trembles a little as she raises the glass. Feet are still in the audience. Not too much shuffling. I look into the mass of faces. There they are. Hands on laps. Knees crossed. People bent like boxes, neatly packed. It is mostly women in the crowd at these things, so you would expect that. No men stretching out their legs, taking the space that is due to them. If a man wants to write a book, he goes out and buys a computer, considers relocating to New York. A woman goes out and takes classes, comes to listen to us lot rattle on. At least this is what one writer teacher friend told me. A lot of us writers teach more than we write. Got to eat. Got to feed our own babies.

How many of these women have children pulling at them with juice-sticky fingers? Does Sybil? I could see her baby, round as a bubble with dark eyes to lap you up. The baby gurgles as Sybil plays with her pens, brushes and pencils. This is in an artist's fantasy. My baby doesn't gurgle, she screams like a jackhammer in the night. Even now my head has trouble staying straight on my neck. I would give up many a fantasy to enjoy just one: to stretch out now on this yawning table. The hard wood may well be a four-poster bed to my wishful bones. I would curl up on it to the tones of this woman humming like a butterfly, press my head into the industrious notebook of the honorary gentleman to my right and rest. They say in the first months there is no such thing as rest. The body of a woman with a child is on high alert even when she is asleep. Perhaps this is why my mind is dribbling now. These faces, this echoing hall, even Sybil may be cloud shadows in a dream, far from the waking world.

The gentleman to my right snuffles his nose into his handkerchief. Sybil is speaking again. I pick up my pen and swing the ink in a swirl the shape of her skirt. My pen keeps drawing patterns: the outline of her head, the bend of her wrist as she holds the book. When I come to her jarrah shoes I pull the heels down into a long stem. She is standing, much like a flower, in the centre. Her hair is shoulder-length; the cinnamon waves just touch the collar of her shirt. I make it cascade the length of the page. It fans out like the petals. She is reading still about the woman with many windows, the one with the wallpaper.

'In this story, the narrator's husband has tried to find a "cure" for his wife's desire to write. Torn between pleasing her family and her need for self-expression, she falls prey to fantasising at great length about the colour and configuration of the wallpaper in her bedroom. At first repulsed by its ugliness, she becomes fascinated by its form. As she writes in her journal…' Sybil pauses again for that serious effect.

'*It is dull enough to confuse the eye in following, pronounced enough to constantly irritate and provoke study, and when you follow the lame uncertain curves for a little distance they suddenly commit suicide – plunge off at outrageous angles, destroy themselves in unheard of contradictions.*'

Commit suicide! A bit melodramatic for a curve. None of my curves appear desperate enough for such an act. I wonder if I can push them over the edge. As the woman reads on, I play with my drawing, sending my easygoing lines careering off the paper. Soon it looks like an explosion has happened right at the base of the stalk out of which Sybil blooms. I am getting excited when I remember I am in front of a crowd. I calm my pen and pretend to take notes in a more orderly fashion. All the while I am making more petals out of her hair. Perhaps some strands could be a waterfall. I sketch in the vine pattern on her skirt and watch as they creep all the way up to her neck. The goblins either side in the margin are grotesque next to the centrepiece Sybil has become. Their eyes bulge out at her, white and deadly. It is as if they are strangled by the vines that have taken off all over the page. They really are as bad as weeds.

'The plight of the woman in this tale is one that cries out against the stultifying oppression of the creative woman, the artist, sculptor, writer. Innumerable stories abound of women's artistic lives cut off at their peak or not even allowed to blossom because their gender does not permit such basic freedom.'

Sybil's pulse throbs against the skin of her throat. A drum banging. She might just start a revolution except when I look out to the crowd, they are blurred in a smudge of charcoal, eyes open, faces closed. I am willing to go along with her, though. She has drawn me in with her suicidal angles and her fervour. It has been a while since I've seen anyone raise a pulse let alone bang a drum.

'It is in this fashion of imprisonment that the narrator of *The Yellow Wallpaper* begins to see women move behind the front pattern of the wallpaper in her bedroom. As Gilman writes, *"The faint figure behind seemed to shake the pattern, just as if she wanted to get out."*'

On the page in front of me, almost black now with my demented scribbling, the figure I have drawn of Sybil opens her eyes. I see the eyelids snap wide, a flash of white. At first I am startled. But then I realise my hand must have moved and drawn eyes when I wasn't looking. Hands have that tendency to fiddle, don't they?

'At night in any kind of light, in twilight, candle light, lamplight, and worst of all by moonlight, it becomes bars! The outside pattern I mean, and the woman behind it is as plain as can be.'

I can see that. I can see how my vines dripping from the ceiling could be perceived as bars. After all, those vines do look like they are strangling the goblins and they do curl up the length of the page. There is no moonlight here, but when I bend my head to the side I can imagine they had grown like that all by themselves. The stalks of my vines in this case could well be bars. I begin to understand what Sybil meant by a top pattern and one underneath. There she is, the image of her I have drawn, staring at me now right through the vine leaves.

Impertinent of her to be so present on the paper! I check to be sure Sybil Jones is still standing onstage. Yes, she is there, humming away, reaching now for her water again. That's the effect of lines drawn close together like that. It achieves the same result that zebras' coats have in the African heat, making the distance shimmer. Disorients the predators. Sybil onstage is still speaking about women writers. I have always been called a 'woman writer'. In my uni days that was quite a thrill. But now, after all these years, you would think we could be 'writers' without the need to tailor the title to our bodies. But then again, you'd think a lot would have happened after all these years.

Byron, for instance, my jackhammer babe. All the relatives brought her pink blankies, nighties, dummies…I have been tempted to say, 'Byron told me she detests pink,' but as she cannot talk, I may have encountered some disbelief. They would have smiled and passed over it as one of my fancies. After all, I am exhausted, and if I did insist on trying to keep working with a young child what more could be expected? I may be oversensitive. Perhaps the blue–pink thing is simply to tell babies apart so no one is embarrassed into mistaking my girl for a boy. Perhaps there is nothing sinister going on at all. I scribble at the goblins' faces.

Sybil's voice softens whenever she stops to read from *The Yellow Wallpaper*. It descends from the drum of her convictions to a whisper as if she has opened a secret passageway and is walking up it in a long silk gown. The hem rustles on the floorboards. She is describing the wallpaper now.

'Looked at in one way, each breadth stands alone, the bloated curves and flourishes – a kind of "debased Romanesque" with delirium tremens *– go waddling up and down in isolated columns of fatuity.'*

I see Byron waddle. At almost one, all her movements are a sort of waddle. Feet thumping in the air, hand pumping as she plays with the coloured balls above her bed. It is an odd thing, to look on something with so much love and in the same breath have to control oneself from running, screaming from the house. Ryan says it's normal. But he has regular hours. He does not get up in the night. He tries to, at least pretends to try, but his effort exhausts me more than doing it myself.

I love the way this Gilman woman paints the husband of the narrator. The husband is kind, caring and utterly useless. By his insistence on her resting without any stimulation he drives her mad. I can tell Sybil finds the depiction delicious. She rolls her tongue around each word when she delivers these bits.

'I get unreasonably angry with John sometimes. I'm sure I never used to be so sensitive. I think it is due to this nervous condition.'

Sybil's lips curl as she gloats over the next line and her eyebrows pinch at acute angles.

'*But John says if I feel so I shall neglect proper self-control; so I take pains to control myself – before him at least, and that makes me very tired.*'

Self-control. How does that song go '*...and I would sell my soul for total control*'? I do not run screaming from the house. As I do not run screaming from this hall. I do not do anything crazy. The only release is this pen in my hand jabbing at the paper in these strange lines that hint at delirium. I have never thought about women before me or women after me. I think of my mum, I suppose, and if she wanted to run screaming. I try to fathom what sort of release she had, if any. I can't come up with anything. She used to garden a lot, endlessly pruning, but isn't that a form of self-control? Cutting all those leaves, trimming those hedges into civilised shapes, no wild patches of grass or thorns. She was manicured, my mum, as much as her lawn.

These women in front of me are the definition of control. But I doubt them. I doubt they are as straight and under wraps as they appear. I stare into the audience. There is one woman, spine stiff against the back of her chair. She hasn't moved all night. She has nodded in all the right places. Even has a book of one of the authors – not mine – on her lap. Occasionally she notes something down on a pocket-sized pad held with her thumb on top of the book. I am sure she will be the first in line to get her book signed. Maybe that was her prime purpose in coming. To have the signature of a real live writer on her very own copy. Her shirt is buttoned right up and her jacket fits firmly around her waist.

I do not buy it for a minute. She dances naked to Arabic music with all the lights out. She makes blood pacts with wolves when the moon summons her. She sneaks into the pattern of the chintz curtains in her bedroom and straddles lovers over the curtain rail. All right, she may not use the curtain rail, but I would swear she has notebooks filled with journal entries or wisps of poems, delightful secrets, dangerous liaisons. Even if they never get to paper, I am sure they are bubbling beneath the brim of that box-cut fringe. I am sure all these women have to hang on tightly to their self-control. I am sure they write something, or would, if they dared. This here is a farce!

I hear the laughter. I look down. My fingers are covered with black ink. My pen has leaked. It has bled all over the page. Rivulets of ink have flooded my vineyards. From the midst of the chaos, Sybil's face emerges as an elfin creature from a forest. Her eyes are lit up. She is laughing at me! I glance up and the woman onstage is still speaking but her form has become ghostly. She moves but her gestures now seem like wisps of clouds. And it is not only her; the audience, the table, the walls, even the faces on either side of me are losing clarity.

As everything around wavers out of its solid shape, my drawing of the woman comes into focus. My Sybil on the page has more dimensions than the one standing by the lectern. In fact, all my scribbling has more life than the scene I had been living only moments before. My vine leaves are wet and thick, a lush jungle. If I put my hand out I am sure the leaves would move and my fingers would feel their cool rubber skins. Now the figure I have drawn peers out from the ropes of vines. She pauses in her laughter. It is that dramatic pause I know well by now.

'Shall we see for ourselves?' The creature on my page speaks. 'Shall we step back and watch these women as they are watching us? Shall we step back a little in time so we get a good running jump onto the stage, into the moment we share now? Them watching you, the renowned writer, watching them?'

The creature on the paper waits for my answer. I am in an uncommon state for one in my profession. I am speechless. The Sybil on my paper trails a finger into the river of ink.

'Shall I begin as all good, if predictable, beginnings do – with a birth?' Raising her finger up to her lips, she licks the tip of it with her tongue. It leaves a thick black streak. Have all my lines and curves hypnotised me? For the moment there is nothing to do but look and listen. I am told that is a good occupation for a writer. In any case, I bet this creature knows how to tell a yarn. Every twist of her elbows, every arch of her eyebrows has a flourish to it. From her inky tongue to her necklace of blackberry vines, she has the flavour of a good storyteller. Animated by an audience, only needing one, it seems, to draw her in, she comes alive. Leaning clean out of the page, she widens her eyes, brushes a strand of cinnamon hair from her face and begins her tale.

'Here it starts. A disc wrapped in skin that slips into my favourite lemon-strung places, the bell, the raven, the king-fisher, the snake, the egg, the feather – what drifts lightly falls hard. I fell hard on this earth, splitting a hundred feathers in my hair, breaking my nails and hitting the bottom of the seabed. Sand in my teeth, weeds in my ears, I stride onto the beach wailing for a warm towel, buttered toast and a cup of tea.'

As a writer I am used to characters jumping out of trains and off ledges to get my attention, but this creature is unlike

11

any vision I have had. How did she find me? I do not speak aloud but she reads my thoughts as if I had.

'And so it begins. I am Sybylla. You were daydreaming, yes? Wondering about all those women at this festival of writers, sitting like boxes, neatly packed? As your thoughts started to open them, unwrap the possibilities, you drew me in. A wandering eye is catnip for a muse of my nature. I am descended from the Sybils themselves, a long line of women trapped in caves, destined for writing on decaying leaves. The holy men of Greece deemed their words too wise for mere women. Their voices must have come from the Gods! My oracular mothers were chained to telling others' destinies while their own fate was fettered to a hole fit for a bear or lion.

'And my mothers became bears and lions. I hear them growling, hissing in the dark, stalking the moon like cloud shadows in the wind. I, too, am destined to stalk like a shadow, free now from any cave, tower, attic, bell jar or other form of savage containment. I hunt for a wandering mind to hear the hissing for the storytelling it is. Now, let me see where you have drawn me.'

The figure on my paper closes her eyes and pauses for a moment as if listening for a barely audible sound.

'Ah...the start of my travels, a hairless child. Shells on my fingers, shells on my toes, I will have music wherever I go. I have landed in a red country, red dirt, the land of girt by sea, a great island between Asia and the Arctic. Gold rays of a hot sun burns the eyes. Maybe it was the wet ink of all that newly minted gold that lisped me into being, who can tell? But my fingers are stained already and small as they are, the bones wriggle. They have a lot on their mind. Let me grab a page now; any page from the wallpaper will let us in...'

Sybylla reaches up from my paper, stretching so far into the air she leaves a black streak from which her body extends. She reaches all the way up to the lectern and tears a page from the leather-bound volume of *The Yellow Wallpaper* that her shadow, Sybil Jones, holds in her hand. Sybil continues talking to the crowd. She does not seem to hear the tearing of a leaf from her book. In fact, no one notices this creature rising out of the sketchpad in front of me. They do not see that both they and Sybil Jones are now transparent as light.

Falling back onto the paper before me, like a genie sucked into a bottle, Sybylla clicks her fingers. I snap to attention. The page she has snatched is spread in front of me. She points to the gaps between the black print.

'There…those blotches of white between the words. If you look close you'll see a morse code. A tapping, a resolute point of entry into a world, hidden but floating visibly when one chances to notice. What if I were the ultimate woman in white slipping from voice to voice, tracing paths with tentacles of observation and memory. Would you follow me?

'What if I presented you with a woman at a table, a kitchen table, elbows squashed between half-peeled potatoes and shelled peas. Carrot skins interfere with the slide of her knuckles across the page crumpled in front of her. She is hurrying as if she is missing a train, she is hurrying like she is catching something, a thread trailed always in front of her face, a carrot of thoughts. She is a horse, a greyhound, a rabbit led by the nose, pelting mindlessly down the road of ink.

'The path opens wide. She is a spot on it. Her face is pale. Her hair dark. There is a vacant look in her eyes. She is somewhere else. I follow her. She does not notice. I bump into her. She mutters an apology. It is a reflex. She does not notice me. I slide into her, soft…a light chill on the back of the neck. She wraps her arms tighter around her.

She wears too much cloth for this heat. A dark dress, trimmed with brown ribbons. Underneath the skirt are layers of petticoats and a pair of drawers. A white collar hovers like a halo around the base of her throat. Together, we walk on.

'We take a right turn off the path and there we are in the middle of bushland. There is dry grass reaching out on a baked flat plain. It is crispy. It crackles as we walk towards a house, snapping at our ankles. Can you see the house? Looming out of the landscape like a boil on the smooth slope of red skin? It sits in the shadow of a hill littered with melaleuca. Fence posts stick in the dirt around it like battered teeth. The lone spark for miles around is the tin roof, a silver dish holding the sun's reflection. The girl waltzes along, through the fence, over the verandah, in the door, across the hallway. As we clatter up the stairs, I creep behind the pattern of her starched lace collar…'

Sybylla looks up at me. Her eyes glint like a spider web in the rain. She beckons, her finger pulling me to her as if we are connected by a thread…

Lucy 1901

The bush smelt so delicious today. The air burnt with eucalyptus and the birds were shrill and gargling, a big party in the trees and I wanted to join them. They get to be gaudy and fly wherever. In spite of the heat, I felt a shiver; as if a wind had struck up and snuck right into my bones. Mother will be so cross if I catch a chill. She's got her hands full as it is, or so she is forever saying.

'Lucy, I've got my hands full enough. Don't you go being idle there, devil's work, devil's work.'

We run around with our hands full so the devil won't come out and grab them. What a peculiar notion! Is he hiding in the bushes all the time? Awaiting empty hands? Mother professes to be awfully religious, God-fearing and all, but she's not. I've seen her glassy face in church and the things she says about people aren't Christian things. She's always got a sharp tongue for her kin as well, and it may be my imagining but it's always us girls who get the force of it while the boys run around free as the birds.

'I've had a hard life,' she says over and over like worn beads on a rosary.

In the quiet of my room, I draw out paper from the pocket of my skirt. I have not written on it since Mother caught me scribbling and told me I shall not have children if I strain my brain like that. But I can't help it. On my walk something got into me – I cannot say…a hissing in my head. Now the paper is an itchy scab and I care naught about anything but scratching it.

I am not going to write silly things. Enough women write silly things. I grew up on romances that would fill anyone with enough hot air to float in one of those big balloons they had at the world fair. Amazing! They sewed it out of silk! A big balloon with enough silk to clothe a hall of ladies. That's what the newspapers said. And all it has got in it is air!

Grandmother and Aunt Mary glare at me from their portraits on my mantle. How they would belt me for saying they and all their romances were full of air. The screwed-up faces they would make. But it is true. It's enough to make a girl with sense wonder if she should go near anything resembling a pen. But I am going to be different. I am different. I can feel it. My brother's tutor, Mr Sharkley, said it himself the other day. The boys were counting out heads of sheep.

'How many sheep would a farmer sell to make one hundred and twenty pounds if each sheep were worth sixty shillings each?'

The boys were at a loss, stuttering 'Well, umm, uh…'

'Forty sheep,' the answer popped out of me before I knew it. Mr Sharkley looked up, his eyes bugging out.

'My word,' he said, 'you are an extraordinary young lady.' Mother looked at me like I had slapped her.

'Go get my hanky, girl,' she snapped. 'What are you doing interfering with the men?'

'Extraordinary!' That is what Mr Sharkley said.

And I am. I'm certainly not like any other girl I know. Sure, it is impressed upon us not to think much, but other girls appear to make an art out of it. And the stuff they churn out, the ladies who claim to write: all the same old plots swung around different ways so the man is chasing the girl and the girl is chasing the boy and that's all they ever do. I'm going to write a proper story like the men. I'm going to write about my own country for a start, not about some Bath or London or some place I couldn't care two tails about.

I'm going to write about the bush like Lawson and Joseph Furphy. I'm going to write so the smell of the gum trees rises off the page. And I am going be real, not fancy. The way the men are real. I am going to write it so they will prick themselves to be sure a girl wrote it. Then maybe they will all take another look at me and think I'm good for more than plodding about the farm and this house.

There goes the bell. What if I pay no heed to it? They'll send Ruthie to fetch me. 'Didn't you heed the bell, girl?'

'Sorry, Father, I was lost in my own world.'

'Your own world?' At this Father guffaws and the rest of the family tinkers in treble behind him. 'You don't have your own world, Lucy. This is it.'

I shrink small as a sparrow under their glares as I bend down to rub his knee, easing his gout.

'What more could a girl want?' I say. None of them catches the irony. They nod happily and harmony settles again over the house like a favourite coat, warming them, suffocating me.

At bedtime I escape back here to my room. It is the best stroke of luck I ever had that Ruth and Ella sleep together and I was granted the attic all to myself. I had a cough one time when I was younger and, fearing it might be influenza, they placed me in the attic. And here I have been allowed to stay. I can say things here that do not get tutted away into insignificance to boil with the kettle or hide beneath the pastry sheets. Here I am worth more than a pair of hands. I have treasures stored up in my room and I unwrap them at night.

The great gums creak in the dark outside my window. Their ghost branches come and wrap around my ankles. All the winds from the many corners of the earth come and play with my hair. I sit up in bed, my legs curled beneath me, and stare into the blackness. I try hard not to blink. I wait until my eyes have that strain to them, then I blink and in that moment I hear it, hissing softly, my name…Lucy…Lucy… Creatures form in the edges of the cupboard, stretching from the cracks in the boards. A voice in the dark and it is calling my name, saying it with so much love it makes me want to cry. My chest swells and my mind opens grand and wild like someone has flipped a lock. I am Pandora and my head is the box!

The strangest pictures – people, faces I have seen as we ride past the poor farms into town, families who walk down the main street – all pour down my bedspread. There is a woman with oranges in her hands. I think her smile is twisted but then I see she has a long scar down the side of her face. Her eyes remind me of the mouth of Father's double-barrelled shotgun. She has so many scars, she says. As I lean forward to grab an orange and beg her to take me into her world, I see a man in the corner of the room. He is half-shaven with sideburns down past his ears. His hat is tilted so I can only see the shadows play on his mouth and chin.

'Do you want me to sing for you?'

The mouth moves but it is like a puppet, out of time with the words. I notice his hands are sweaty and smudged with dirt. He starts to belt out a tune so mournful it wrenches through the air like the dingo's wail. I bend my head to see if I can peep beneath the brim of his hat. As I do, I notice a child in a nightie squatting on the floor. Her eyes draw me. They are purple.

'I be Violet,' she says.

She is tiny, more of a small cat than a human. 'You have no shoes on,' I say. 'Are you cold?'

A wave of motherly instinct seizes me. I want to cover her up and hold her close. I reach to lift her up. She closes her fingers around my waist. The man is still singing. He is shuffling his feet from side to side, thrusting his head back and forth like an emu. The woman with the oranges is rocking too, back and forth. She throws an orange in the air as if she will start juggling while the man bangs his feet on the floor. Streaks of orange paint the corners of the room.

In the light of the orange skins, I see a crowd of figures huddled there, awaiting their turn to come out: a small foot with a silver buckle, a neck with a pale-yellow choker...My room is like the Fitzgerald's Circus that sprang up in Mr Darcy's field last summer. I have so many questions for my characters. Why do you bang your feet? Where are your eyes? What are those scars? Why have you no shoes?

I reach across to my bedside table and fumble with the stump of wax I filched from the storeroom. The matches jump around my fingers in my rush to light one.

'Hurry, hurry, hurry,' the hissing says, 'you have to catch them all.'

At last I get the candle lit, pull out the scraps of paper I pinched and scribble. I write them all down, or most of them at least. The shadows in the corner wait their turn. I start with the orange woman, Clara. She talks for hours. She has so many scars, so many stories. She caresses each scar as if it were a pet while she speaks.

'They are my babes,' she tells me and one by one we trace them down her body. The tuneless man is quieter. He speaks now with a whimper more than a wail. Violet says nothing but she clamps onto me tight and tells me her shoes are filled with water. I catch them in ink. My words are clumsy but they hold them there. I write until the sun lights up the dust in the air. I hide the pages in my Bible and stow it under my mattress. They are jammed now between the Little Lord Jesus and Moses. I hear Maggie drag the wood to the kitchen humming 'Rosie Darling' and I am thrown back into the waking world of pans, chickens, sheep and chores.

I will think of my creatures between feeding hens and ironing the sheets. I'll make them so true, they'll pepper the pages with the sounds of the bush. I'll tie the heart of this land down: all the squatters' wives with nothing but dust to bake with, battling alone in huts in the middle of the queerest places where kookaburras laugh at them and their children are swept away in floods. Floods here spring out of drought. Everything in this land is extreme and there is no give, no mercy at all. Just like that story of the Murphys' child down by Brownstone Creek.

I've got it! The orange woman, the one I saw sitting on the bench outside the town store last Sunday, the one I remembered last night. She was peeling an orange. She was sobbing. That's why she cries. She lost her child in a flood, the same flood as that Murphy woman. A story of a mother and child caught in a flood. A true bush tale that pinches the reader in the guts. You think there is no sense, it is foolish imagining, but then the pieces fall and there you have it, a tale to tell. Like a dream abandoned in the starkness of the morn, only to find it foretold a death or a birth.

The story grows thicker in my head as I iron. The rhythm of my hand as it follows the nap of the sheet serves my thoughts. By the time the ironing is done I have the thread of my story down. It sits and waits there in that crease between Father's shirt collar and the orange peel collecting at my feet.

It is late afternoon now and I am stiff and sore. Even the daily chores are wearing me so thin I feel fit to snap. And all the while the hissing voice in my head is turning to a roar. I am folding the linen and all I can hear are Clara and Violet and the tuneless man. I think of them jammed between the pages of my Bible. Maybe Violet is dabbling her feet in a stream. I'm sure they have those in the Bible, not that I can recall any. There are great floods and oceans but I am sure there are streams as well and there are certainly shepherds. That's a nice thought, Violet with a gentle shepherd, herding sheep much like we do…Christ's little children. Mother casts me dark looks from her place by the window. She always sits by the window darning holes, needle quick as a silverfish. Her tongue too is a needle.

'Lucy, what are you up to, girl? You've used too much starch in those sheets, wandering child! More hindrance than help! Give that sheet to Maggie.'

I pass the sheet over to Maggie, who gives me such a kind look I could cry right there and then. Mother hasn't finished yet.

'What's wrong with you, girl? You look fatigued. What have you been up to?'

'Nothing, Mother. I could not sleep well 'tis all.'

'Not reading?' Her glasses slide down her nose.

'No, Mother.'

'None of that scribbling?' Her voice reaches a piercing note as the appalling thought occurs to her.

'No, Mother.'

'Your eyes are red. Maggie, are her eyes not red?'

'They look right enough to me.' Maggie's soothing voice does nothing to calm Mother. If anything it heightens her condition.

'I'm not going mad, Maggie. I would swear by St Christopher her eyes are red! Lucy, you are sixteen, ripe for a man to make you his bride, and what man desires a woman with a head full of nonsense? Girls with your temperament are a burden on their mothers, on their families and on any man unfortunate enough to take one in.'

'Yes, Mother.'

'Poor Maude Davis's daughter got her head into books — not lady's books but books she stole from her brothers, deceitful child that she was. She wasted away, there and then. Nothing poor Maude could do! Soon the girl was thin as a stick and carrying herself with airs. Her mind went roving. A woman's mind is not meant to hold such notions. Lost in anguish, she was, before she lost her senses! Maude was inconsolable, wouldn't come out of her house for a month, and that kind Father John had to go and comfort her out of her misery. Do you want that for your own Mother, girl?

'I tell you, I've not slept well. That is all.'

Mother puffs back down on her chair like I've seen the roosters do after a good morning's crowing. 'Fetch your sisters, girl. It's time for tea.'

I run out into the yard. I could run and run and keep on running. Maude Davis has three daughters and I never heard of a fourth who drove herself mad. I am running and running so hard, I don't see Mr Sharkley until I barrel straight into him.

'Whoa there, child. Are you being chased by Dante's demons?'

'Only my mother,' I say, and we laugh.

He has a sweet laugh, a kind of singsong tone. It reminds me of the birds in the bush.

'Better Dante's demons!' he says.

'And who is Dante that he has demons all his own?'

'You know, it is a pity,' he says, 'to have a mind like a sponge and nothing but frippery to fill it. You have more in you than your brothers combined.'

More in me than Will and Fred! I give Mr Sharkley my most winning smile.

'A freak,' he says, 'quite a freak of nature.' He glances at me once more, then shuffles past.

I could well crumble into the gum leaves at my feet. The air sails out of me in one long sigh. I cannot abide myself. Perhaps I do belong in Fitzgerald's Circus.

'Pretty as a daisy, my girl Maisy. Pretty as a daisy, my girl Maisy.' My sisters' chanting reaches me as I near the river. They are skipping in unison with the rhyme, long hair swinging golden as butter in the afternoon light. The rope is moving so quick beneath their feet, it encases them in a white blur. Their chant carries on and on. The rhythm echoes the singing man. I see him again, shuffling his boots to his tuneless drone.

The white skipping rope contrasts with their yellow plaits. Behind them the river glides past like a silver snake, as much a part of the rhyme as their skipping. The thick ropes of the river, the hair, the skipping string weave into one. I feel my own body covered in ropes, the chords of my own hair wrapping around my wrists. Everything – the place, my family, the battering sun – holds me down fixed to that spot. I cannot move. I cannot breathe.

'What is it, Luce?'

They stop their skipping. Their forms waver in the heat. I shade my eyes to see their faces. My oldest sister, Ella, is watching me, cheeks drawn in. Beside her my younger sister, Ruthie, gawks, mouth open.

'You look so strange,' Ella says.

I draw myself out of my reverie. 'It's just the heat. Come on in, it's time for tea.' Ruthie cocks her head to the side,

'Don't worry, Ella, Luce is always odd.' Ruthie has inherited my mother's sharp tongue and isn't one to let anything go without letting a barb loose. Ella shakes her head at Ruthie. As we walk back to the house, Ella and Ruthie chat gaily about Sunday's picnic.

'Are you wearing that green dress, Ruthie? You look so pretty in that one.'

'Yes, I thought I'd wear it with Mamma's rose hat. She bought it for herself but it looks far more fetching on me.'

'The rose will look delightful. I wonder if the Woodbridge's son has returned from Melbourne.'

'Friday, I think. I knew you liked him, Ella. You went bright red when we were at church that time and he picked up your hymn book.'

'Well, he does have a way about him. A gentleman, not like Will or Fred.'

On they chat, dresses and boys, hats and gloves and which with which and who with whom. It is their whole life.

'You'd look fine in that yellow dress of Ella's for the picnic,' Ruthie says now to me. 'We just need to take it out a bit at the waist.' She is having another jab.

'Yes, the yellow dress would be fine.'

I am thicker around the waist. Mother yanks my stays so tight I cannot breathe, but I still do not make a fine shape. Nor do I have Ruth's fine hands or Ella's delicate lashes. Nor do I work on using my lashes the way Ella does when either the country boys or the gentlemen are around. I do genuinely admire the way she makes them flutter, though – like humming bird's wings.

When I see myself in the glass, it is not that I have an aversion to what I see; I simply cannot see myself without wondering what everyone else sees. Nothing is certain. For instance, Father said I had genteel hands, and then Will said they were farmer's hands. The same with my face. My Aunt Rosie said I was an appealing creature. Then I happened upon Ella declaring it was a pity I was so plain. When I look in the glass it always changes in keeping with what I heard last. I don't have much of a notion what I look like except for the basics: brown hair, pale skin with lots of freckles from the sun and hazel eyes. Mother tries to bleach my freckles with lemon juice. Bad enough to be a girl but a plain girl! It would have been a mercy to drown me at birth like the kittens last spring.

'Ruth, don't scamper. Walk nicely like a lady.'

I can hear Mother as Ella and I enter the dining room.

We each have our place: my two brothers on one side of the table, us girls on the other. Mother says grace and it is always sufficiently full of her suffering and what a duty it is to persevere. On this night, Mr Sharkley is our guest, as happens when lessons run over time.

As grace finishes, Maggie sets down a leg of boiled mutton on the table followed by two bowls with mountains of peas and carrots. Father cuts the meat. By the time it is my turn, which is second last before Ruthie, most of the good cuts are gone and he is scraping the bone and fat. Talk around the table follows a well-trodden path each night: farm work, the next trip to town or next picnic. Mother prods Father into talking about the sheep, the market for the sheep and how the boys need to learn more about sheep.

This evening, I am so tired I rather enjoy the drone of the men's voices, pierced occasionally by Mother's high one. I let myself wander back to the creatures in my room. They are waiting for me like delicious treasures. I watch the gravy boat as it tips over our plates and the gravy pours in a stream like muddy water...foaming...foaming brown water...the current plummeting past wood piles and branches. I am in the flood with Clara the orange woman and Violet...I can see them both, faces blanched white as the mashed potato, and the water is rising so quickly. It is climbing up the legs

26

of chairs, rain swooping down on their little house as if it were an ant hill in the massive sway of the valley. The trees are sticks. The land has turned miniature, and giant waves are riding down through ditches and roads that have always been so safe, so familiar. The water chases Clara and Violet higher. They move from chairs to tables to the roof of their shed. How quickly barren soil becomes a river!

Cows bleat mournfully as the flood pushes them past, eyes cracked with fear. The family dog, Red, is scraping to climb onto the roof. His eyes, so trusting, are fixed on Clara as his lower body sinks further and further into the water. She clamps harder onto Violet…Can she shift a little to the left and help him up, just an inch or so to find his footing? Violet, a wraith in her arms, is stunned. Her eyes watch in horror as the cows, the saucepans, the wheel from the shed, pass her in a strange dream. It cannot be real.

Red whines in fear, paws scraping frantically for a hold on the roof. Red had been there when Violet was born. Red has licked Clara's face every morning for the past seven years. She cannot bear to watch him drown like this. For just an instant, Clara thinks, if I just stretch this way…and Violet slides against the bark. She is down and under, her head nodding in the water. Clara stares out into the foam and has to hold herself from leaving all the pain to come, jumping in and following her daughter down into the mud where nothing is remembered and nothing need be forgiven. They find Violet's shoes three days later, washed up near the McCulloughs' place.

'Lucy, Sharkley here says you're outdoing the boys at arithmetic!' Father is staring, his chin cloaked in the turkey folds of his neck.

Everyone's attention is fixed on me. The blood rushes to my face. I choke back tears at the thought of Violet being washed, a rag doll on the water. I have to write it all down. I ache to run up to my room and get it down quickly, before it deserts me and I have only the shell of a story left on the paper.

'I cannot fathom how it occurred. Forty sheep simply popped into my head.'

'Lord, you are a marvel, Lucy,' Father chuckles. At this everyone relaxes and titters in the background. 'Mr Sharkley, have you ever made the acquaintance of such a girl?'

Mr Sharkley grins at me. 'No, Sir, I fear I have not had that pleasure.'

I bow my head down, eyes tracing the lace of the tablecloth.

'Give Lucy another number, Sharkley,' says Father. I look up in time to see him wink.

'All right, then, I shall. Lucy, what would one have left if thirty-five sheep were subtracted from fifty-one?'

'I could not say.'

'Luce, give it a try!' Ella nods at me.

'Why are we bothering?' Will chimes in. 'Where has the pudding got to?'

'Sorry, I cannot say what it might be.'

'Leave the girl alone,' Mother says. 'Lucy is far too engaged with her chores to have a mind for such things.'

'I was going to say, Sharkley, the local country school the girls attend is outdoing your private tutoring of the boys. What would you have said to that?'

Father enjoys humiliating Mr Sharkley. I imagine it is his lack of education, having made his money off his own toil, 'the fat of the land' as he puts it, that makes him want to roast an educated man who knows four languages including French and Latin.

'The local schools are well and good,' says Mr Sharkley, 'but one can hardly compare them to private tutelage for boys. Lucy here, it is plain, was merely guessing.'

'Right you are, Sharkley, right you are. I only hope they don't stuff too much in our girls' heads. It is a dangerous thing and, as that Dr Clarke says, what happens when their brains outgrow their natures? Let them be literate – no one likes a daft woman, and they can amuse themselves with letters about fads – but as for more…I do wonder at the sense of it!'

'Indeed, indeed,' says Mr Sharkley. 'I did have a lady show me her scribbles once. I think she had ambitions of writing, you know. It was dreadful, filled with dressmaking, baby minding, even recipes.'

'Like that Lawson woman puts about?'

'Yes, much like that *Dawn* rubbish.'

'Don't go rubbishing *The Dawn*, Mr Sharkley, I have some excellent recipes from that. You might be eating one right now. Maggie, bring the pudding out, please.'

'Sure enough, Mother, sure enough,' Father says.

Maggie places the pie dish in the centre of the table. Now everyone is far more engrossed in filling themselves than in worrying about *The Dawn*, or me for that matter. At last I escape to my room, pleading a headache. Mother gives me a look like a crow spying a mouse as I excuse myself. My performance at dinner did not put her off the scent.

What do I care now? I think as I shut the door and my room opens out into my patch of freedom. I stay up late into the night, scribbling down the story of Clara losing Violet in the flood and now selling oranges down the main street of Brownstown. The singing man is her husband, I decide. He has been away for a week before the flood, buying stock. At the loss of his child he has become a drunkard. I never see his eyes; they remain shaded and a part of me is thankful for that. He says he is to blame for leaving a woman alone in the bush. All men know a woman cannot be trusted.

Clara takes it upon herself. 'But an inch,' she mutters as she peels her orange skins, 'but an inch.'

They are trodden down with guilt. It gets between them like a tick, growing bloated on their sadness. Night after night I pen their story. This is no recipe of love, blooming roses and grand gestures. I write it as though I am reporting it for *The Bulletin*, sparse and hard. I write it in the style of the bush stories the men write. For weeks after I am like an expectant mother as ever so carefully I copy out the story onto proper paper. I purchased it in secret with Maggie's help from the town store. I determine I will call my story simply, 'The Flood of Brownstone Creek'.

What woman has written like this? None that I know of. Am I a freak like the Bearded Lady from the circus? Who was I to have such pretensions? These fears creep into my room, overshadowing my creatures and all their stories. Doubt at my own foolishness grows in me much like that tick, fatter and fatter till I have to force myself to hold my pen and get the story down.

I keep it locked in my drawer for the next month. I am uncertain now what must be done. Should I claim it as my own? It sends chills through me to think of my name there, all embossed. But if I put my name, will any publisher look at it? Will they read my writing differently? Will they laugh like my Father and Mr Sharkley did that night at dinner? Will I be performing, a freak to them as well? It sits there waiting for me. I dream of it when I am stooped over the clothes wringer or dusting the shelves. Every moment now seems to carry great import. It is my child. Now I am on that roof, surrounded by the flood. Do I cast it away? A good mother would release it so it could live. A man's name might work...After all, it will be read so much better that way, and do I not want it read like a man's writing, firm and robust, not fanciful? I choose Luke – it is a biblical name and close to Lucy at least – and Finch. Like the bird. I like the sound of that: Mr Luke Finch. He sounds far superior to Lucy Franklin. I sign it, a swirling signature alive with promise.

Just the other day, I eavesdropped on the boys' lessons and heard Mr Sharkley telling them about the Greeks and their Trojan horse. Mr Finch will ride like the Greeks rode their horse into Troy. A whole army lay waiting in its wooden belly. But I will not be found. No, Lucy will be secret.

Between the Chapters...

I cannot lift my eyes from Sybylla and the delirious patterns that have swamped my paper. If I am not asleep then she has cast a spell.

'See, your leaking pen has made a river through our vineyard.'

Sybylla points to my vine leaves drooping from the top of the paper. Between them is a splash of ink. It makes its way in an accidental fashion until it spills over the edge onto the table.

'Perhaps it's the creek from Lucy's story,' says Sybylla. 'Don't you love that trickling sound? Constant movement. Never in the same river twice, they say. The Celts measure time in this way; a fluid element, tangible. They love to bathe in it.'

I recall reading about the Celtic otherworld. The faerie realm had its own river of time constantly crossing the flow of time in this world, changing the humans who were touched by its spirit. To enter the faerie realm was to step outside earthly time into quite another stream of existence.

Sybylla holds out the page of *The Yellow Wallpaper* she has torn from the book of Sybil Jones.

'Did you like Lucy? In walking through the gaps between the words of *The Yellow Wallpaper*, we have crept behind the pattern. Lucy is only the first of the women we must meet who have been lost inside it. There are more to come. Let us imagine we are meandering beside this river of time, a part of nature as much as the mountains, the forests and the weeds. Let us follow it a while. I do love water. I landed in the sea, you know.'

'But what about Lucy?' I can't believe we would leave her here, just on the cusp of stardom.

'Lucy, Lucy quite contrary, how does your garden…we are finished with the best part of that story. Lucy found stardom…of a sort. To begin with, 'The Flood' was hailed as a gripping yarn with immense vision. Virile writing, they said, full of vigour and all that stuff. The wheel quickly turned when the papers dug up the real Luke Finch. The wrath of the critics at being fooled by a girl was boundless. They accused her of mimicking men with all the prowess of a well-trained monkey. One went so far as to say her slippery deception was sourced in the tongue of Eve with which all women are endowed and all men are cursed to contend. How fast the fall from visionary to monkey, and all in the glide of the slippery slide between one's legs.

'Some said they knew all along a girl wrote it. They delighted in their new pet. A real Australian girl they called her. She was hailed for her gutsy bush courage. Norman

Lindsay himself remarked on her pert rump. Her family disowned her, saying great shame had been heaped upon their name. She barely survived their wrath. They lay claim to her, however, when as ailing parents they needed a daughter to wash their backs and scrub their toenails. Hardly a brilliant career.' Sybylla picks up her stride.

Thank God it is better now. I have myself been called a virile writer but that's a compliment, isn't it? I mean, in this day and age women *can* be virile. Or am I fooling myself? All this walking and thinking makes me hot. I take off my shoe and trail my foot in the river. So icy! My toes turn a shade of blue. I let the cold in.

The audience likes us writers young and beautiful. We are performers of a sort. I can see how a young girl even back then would attract all that hype. I catch my reflection in the water. Strands of red hair have escaped from the elastic. They frame my face, making it look wistful. At thirty-nine I still have life in me; shelf life, that is. I could buy a sporty car, one of those bubble ones, to boost my image. It would be egg-yolk yellow or gold as the rings on a bee, the colour of danger in the wild, but I don't know if the baby seat would fit in one.

It is getting harder to be a recluse these days. They draw us out with photo shoots, public debates, interviews...I had a young girl come to interview me last week. She wore a turquoise disc around her neck. To free up her throat chakra, she said. So many questions. I said I was very bad at these things. She said I was wonderful. I found myself talking so much my throat was dry. Perhaps I was lonely that day.

It can be lonely, a book and a baby. None of your species to talk to. I saw a documentary on prisoners in isolation.

Apparently they scratch their heads so much they can dig a hole in it without knowing. That's how I feel at times, sitting at my computer. The screen glares back. We have a staring competition. I wonder why I never finished law. I scratch my head.

Prisoners do lots of repetitive movement. My fingers move over and over. I reach for my green tea. My fingers move again. The phone rings. At times it is the best sound in the world. An escape hatch. Other times, it is pure evil, taking me away from the hole in my head. I let it ring and ring, buzzing till it is dead.

The baby I cannot ignore. But she is baby world. We watch baby television. Lots of music and bright colours. I go from isolation to an asylum where everything is oversized and happy, happy, happy. I jump around the room. I am a frog. She laughs. I have no dignity. I forget how to speak in whole words. Sometimes I forget myself. While she sleeps I am back at my computer. I write words like hoochy, coochy. They are fun but a whole book of this may be ahead of our time.

It is difficult to have your writing hinge on the sound of a baby crying. Every second of silence is precious metal. What would Chekhov or Tolstoy do? Would they write the disruption into their Great Russian classics…*and then Ivanovich heard a ghastly wail*? The baby would become background setting and be found by a passing stranger three days later, starving and pale, an ideal orphan for a tragedy. The child deserted by Anna Karenina! It is these odd thoughts one has in isolation, hypnotised by the hole in one's head, tapping the keys in repetition, listening for one's own private orchestra to sound. And when the music starts, you know for sure you have gone mad. It is a sweet freedom, one you crave like a junkie long deprived.

The click of Sybylla's jarrah heels is faint in the distance. I come out of my reflection and push through a jungle of leaves till I reach her. She is walking with purpose. She has followed the river to the point where it flows into the ocean. I can hear the waves and taste the salt in the air. I am out of breath as I catch her.

'Just around this bend is the beach. By my bird's eye I can spy a speck out there upon the ocean. I suppose it makes sense, really. We have travelled almost thirty years along our river from the turn of the Golden Age. Where else would you expect to find a woman with an itch for ink in this dry land but all out at sea? Before we embark on this journey,' she spins around to hold me in her dark gaze, her pond eyes luminous, 'be warned. There is no beginning or end that may suit this tale. There is only a wind here and a hole that may swallow you up, so stick close and, whatever you do, try not to drown.'

Sybylla kicks off her heels and strips off her clothes. She sprints over the sand and dives into the ocean. Her body glimmers, a shock of silver in the air before she is in the waves. I have no choice but to follow. We swim for what seems like eternity until even I can see there is a figure in the water. It is a woman. She is not struggling but floating. If it were not for all this distance to the shore I would think she was having a fine time bathing.

The woman does not seem surprised to see us. She greets us with a wave, a lazy lift of the hand and a smile, taut across her face. She has a beautiful face: cheekbones high, with gold hair in kiss-curls around each ear. Her eyes are as green as the ocean around us, lidded like a cat's. She begins to talk, chatting casually in the tone of a light luncheon. She does not stop talking. Perhaps no one has swum by here for a while. I think she is lonely. We float alongside and I take care to watch out for any winds. I, for one, have no intention of drowning.

Vera 1929

I was sitting on the beach when I realised I had nothing behind me so the only way was ahead and there sat the sea, a big waiting goblet and I was thirsty, as I have been all my life and never sated. Now you know where it ends, where, you may ask, does it begin? I tell you I had it all: looks, brains, talent – perhaps all was too much. My looks ensnared me more than any other. My brain meant I thought far more than was wise till I trapped myself with my own intellect. As for my talent, well, that was the thing that caused the trouble in the first place, the hissing at my heels for me to be heard, 'cause I must be heard and if I was heard properly, I was convinced all would bow down in contrition at my great genius.

Determined as I was and assisted always by the great man himself, Dr Sigmund Freud, I steeped myself in psychoanalysis and pickled myself in alcohol. You could say I had a father complex. I would say I had a 'man' complex. I insisted, you see, on getting a word in at whatever cost. In this time and with the men I'm talking about, the cost is always greater than one can or should afford.

I lived in a world mothers warn their daughters about. It is a world of dark corners.

'Don't go in there, don't go in there.'

Mothers tuck their children in safe and sound, with lullabies perhaps: 'You be a good girl. Good girls don't behave like that, good girls don't go to places like that, they don't dress like that or the devil men with their horny feet and lustful loins will find you. They'll gobble you up for tea and spit you out all ground up.'

My own mother died from a miscarriage when I was three. All I remember of her are milky hands lifting me up and the smell of vanilla mixed with sea salt. We had lived by the sea before moving to the city after she died. That is why I am called back here. I was born to its song and it is only fitting it should sing my requiem.

I had a father, needless to say. Daddy wasn't one to care much about dark corners. In fact, he inhabited them frequently himself. I do suspect that, even if Mother had not died, I would still have yearned for those dark corners. Are they in you? Those dark places when you are born? Do some have them darker than others? Those dark places were the centre of the world as far as I was concerned. At Betsy's and Theo's in Sydney, the heart of Bohemia revelled between the piss in the alleys and the grog they served on the sly, since the wowsers brought in six o'clock closing. We drank the fruit of the vine for breakfast and believed ourselves the finest thinkers in all this southern land.

I had better amend that a little. That was not an inclusive 'we'. I was not included in the intellectual element of the movement. I was better known for my legs, or 'ladders to Venus' as they were called. It was a joke among the lads, how often they were climbed, and many a wit would ask if I needed the steps fortified. How did I end up there, a walkway for the self-appointed gods of the day? It was the only place any thought, any 'real' art, happened in this country at all. I was born to be an artist. What other cradle would I seek?

Other women pined for a breath of the air I drank nightly, the immense conversations, the comparison of all the great artists – Rubens, Raphael, Marlowe, Shakespeare – and all the talk of Rome, Athens, Cairo, Constantinople! Our lads had been places in the Great War and their eyes grew huge as they spoke of spices and silk markets and women, dark as the natives here, who move their bellies like snakes to drums and wailing flutes. All these wonders mixed in with mustard gas and rats! But not all women would come into those cafes where I drank and danced, kicking 'Venus' so high that the patrons would salivate into their mugs. The price of respectability was boredom, an island of a sort or, as I saw it, a fragrantly padded cage.

Not for me the gilded cage. I had been born with poetry for blood. Daddy ruled the stage of my life from the time I could crawl. He travelled continents. He was the avowed king of poets, followed permanently by a mass of young men quivering in his shadow, quivering to be him. And what would be more natural but that I should be his queen? Things didn't follow as planned. In trying to engage the attention of that band of followers, I found myself hauled to the children's court on charges of sexual perversion. None of the merry band accompanied me.

This is where I had the pleasure of meeting Dr Sigmund for the first time, in theory, not flesh. They called in an expert who said my behaviour, according to the great man himself, was a clear case of sexual perversion in a twelve-year-old girl. It turned out that I had seduced the poor boy in question into divesting me of my virginity. The magistrate made a note of my nervous manner (what child wouldn't be so in a court of law!), and decreed that I, Vera Brandon, was of shifty character. He warned of lust and the sinfulness of such desires.

At the time, I made of it a fervent poem of how woman's nature is torn asunder beneath the microscope of male analysis. It was tragic in both content and form, so I will not bore you with it now. I protested often on the effect of Freud on the sexual freedom of women. All around hailed my passion, but it was the allure of sexually free women they cheered. The men were fond of perceiving themselves as dastardly satyrs, the very depiction of all that made those mothers tremble. They talked of their pursuit of young virgins, marked their victories with rounds of beer and fancied themselves well endowed in every way. I can attest to the fact that many of them were not. The budding Rimbauds I had thought them to be quickly lost their potency. I could not say exactly when the magic faded for me. I had been flying in my fairytale land where I was a great poetess surrounded by like minds. Just when the glass cracked and I started aching for oblivion, I cannot be certain.

The fish are nibbling at my toes – an odd sensation. Or is it my imagination that I am surrounded by sucking mouths, wanting more, wanting every part of me? My eyes are burning with salt. What a strange fish I make. White crystals drying around my mouth, in the cracks of my lips, my tongue baking in its casing. I am not so pretty now, hey?

Fingers fish bait in the water, my mouth's a hook will skew any dull fish...See, I'll open wide and all my bones prick your jelly eyes...See, I can spin rhyme. I've been spinning them all my life. Spin, spin, spin...A hapless little spider.

My eyes were so closed when it all began and I thought I knew everything. I would be happy to die young and bloody, with my name remembered years after as a sorceress of men, a mighty poetess in the realms of Sappho herself, with a pitchfork tongue that scalded and caressed every ear laid bare to it. That would be me: young, vain and glorious. I would take on the darkness, swallow it, ferment in it and grow mighty on its juices...a Persephone who eats her pomegranate and smacks her lips. I would rule Hades. I would not arise at springtime.

Often I walked down around the ferry wharves of Sydney Cove contemplating my destiny as a poetess. The richness of words would heave in my head like the ocean and I would scrawl down verse upon verse. One time when I was walking, I thought of dropping into the cold water and washing myself clean, washing away all the dirt I had accrued in those dark places...like a baptism. I remember that from church. My Aunt Josie took me when I was young. She often tried to take me places but Daddy said she was interfering. Soon she stopped coming. She died in the influenza epidemic after the war.

But I loved church. Church was romantic. It dealt in all my favourites: death, redemption, ecstasy. If I hadn't become a whore, who knows, I might have been a nun. After all, given the men I've had, God wouldn't be such a bad choice. I could flagellate myself, prostrate myself on hard floors, gaze endlessly on the sprawled naked body of Christ, blood dripping into rose bowls. Ecstasy. Yes, there would have been quite enough drama for me in that setting. Surprising how close the comparisons could be to the life I've led. But I digress. Where was I? By the river. How fitting. My taste for tragedy appeared insatiable. I was imagining myself as Ophelia floating so divinely, dragged down by layers of velvet.

I wrote a poem instead of plunging into the water. I wrote a poem conveying the eroticism of death, the passion of one's last step taken not unconsciously, but fully knowing and finding, at last, the final liberation. I wrote it as a woman scorned by all the men she had known:

> *Ah, let me sing my poet's song…*
> *My jagged body is a ship's broken hull,*
> *I have beached myself upon the rocks…*
> *All the sailors who boarded me with desire must drown,*
> *their skulls smooth like mine,*
> *crack in time to the splintering of my whalebone heart…*

I hear echoes of Zora Cross. She is a favourite poetess of mine.

> *Woman, pausing on the marble stair,*
> *Come down one…come down two;*
> *Death is creaking through the doors of air.*
> *And a red, red knife for you.*

Wonderful! She had a poet's soul. She writes only for little ones now, I hear, after she was devoured by the carnivore critics for lurid prose unsuited to a lady. Like the mainstay of my sex, her passion is wasted on burping babes – stuff a dummy in her mouth, give her a rattle. I prefer a cleaner end. But did I not say I loved tragedy, and that's about as tragic as it gets. I drift, I drift...but drifting can be as good as driftwood. I could have used some driftwood. I did not jump in that water. No, no. Rather, I folded my poem up, placed it in my pocket and walked past the wharfies with their smutty cackles and crab hands, back up Young Street, into Bridge Street...

'How pretty you are, young miss.' His voice curves round the bend.

I cannot see him yet but he has spied me, there from his dark arbour beneath the sign for aspirin.

'You may play the bow to my fiddle.' And there he is, eyebrows lifted, a Pan with a bottle of cheap brandy in his hand.

'Why, Sir, how you do pounce on a poor maid!'

'A maid, are you a maid tonight? I must have mistaken you for a gypsy of a girl I know. My deepest apologies. I will never seek to tempt you again.'

'Don't you be going anywhere with that brandy, Jack.' I reach for his elbow and keep pace with him as he turns to walk down George Street.

'Ah, I knew the call of nectar would never fall on deaf ears. What are you doing wandering, my shepherdess, on this the night of the grand ball? Surely my lady should be primping and frilling before the throng comes to dine in Arcadia tonight?'

That's right, it was the night of the Artists' Ball…Maybe that is why I wander down this way…the night the glass began to warp…

'I will be no shepherdess tonight, Jack. I will be a mermaid.'

'A mermaid!' Jacks eyes light up as he thinks of me as a mermaid, all scales and flesh. 'My slippery little girl, and may I be your merman?'

'Jack, this mermaid swims alone.'

'Ah, my sweet, why is it my hell that I cannot afford you? You swing always an apple from a bough before my eyes.'

Jack throws an arm around my shoulders. He has had the best part of the brandy. The velvet of his coat rubs against my skin. It has a green sheen, giving his face a sallow look, like moss shining at the bottom of a dank puddle. Jack is far from the fresh young lad from Brisbane he once was. He tripped into Sydney two years ago, full of song and poetry. Then I had thought there may be hope with him…He might be my friend, the first to pierce the mask of my beauty that seemed to blind so many men. But I was destined to be Medusa always, it seems, locked away in my cold-stone stare.

'Jack, have you seen this week's issue of *Jones' Weekly*?'

'Not yet, darling, why?'

'I sent some poems in a while ago. I thought maybe this week…I have a new one here, Jack. I just wrote it down by the wharves.' I pull the poem out of my pocket.

'Are you going to be topless, Vera?'

'Almost, I'm using veils. It is a poem about the passion of a woman as she takes her last step, like a dagger plunging or, in this instance, a shipwreck. Would you like to hear it?'

'A shipwreck, you say? That reminds me of something I read…I've been writing so much myself, living like a monk.

It will be good to pay homage to Bacchus tonight. Will your nipples show through?'

'No, Jack, the imagination has to do some work.'

'What a shame. I thought I would go as the little tramp, seeing as it suits my wardrobe so well. See, what do you think of my walk?' Jack hobbles out in front of me in a woeful imitation of Chaplin.

'Jack, you look somewhere between a duck and a lame beggar.'

'A beggar...ahh...I could go as a beggar man. That would also suit my wardrobe and my circumstances, a beggar as I am for your affection! Hey, we're almost at Theo's. Shall we dip in here to wet our whistle before the big night?'

I tuck the poem back in my pocket.

We make our way down Campbell Street to the dirty green door. Every time you turn into this street it is an archway into another world. The Chinese quarters always plunge you into the heart of something foreign yet so close, somewhere between a nightmare and your strangest fantasy. Eyes soaring on opium wings drift past. The stench of the place – roasting pork, sewage and steam – fills your senses so that the green door appears as the entrance to the Underworld. We give the secret signal with the bell: one long ring and two short ones. Theo's eyeball presses close to the peephole. The door swings open and Jack and I follow Theo's hulk up a stairway, feeling our way in complete blackness. At last we come to a drawn curtain. As Theo pulls it back, the light and noise crash onto us as if we have been spat out of the birth canal.

Most of the patrons are already in fine form, dressed in their costumes for the ball. Already some are up swinging to jazz tunes belting from the music box. As I make my entrance with Jack, I catch eyes and hold them locked on my bow lips before they slip down my silk stockings. Jack heads off to collect more nectar. And there is Daddy in the corner, surrounded by his legions of flies. 'And here comes the queen bee herself,' he hails me with a long exhale. I slide lazily to his side, drooping an arm around his shoulders.

'Hello, Daddy dearest,' I breathe husky in his ear.

The flies gather deeper around us, their precious honey pots. I take Daddy's hand and we swing slowly to the strains of 'Squeeze Me'. They watch every sway of my hips, every rocking movement I make. Daddy's hand presses the small of my back. Springtime is far away now. As the song fades out, the flies come and tell me how I inspire their desire, how I am a goddess, how I will be their next portrait, their next play. Their salutations vary depending on their sobriety.

'Vera, you have split my heart tonight,' says Tom, an artist with a propensity for drawing naked women pursued by any number of rapacious beasts.

'You are a divine flame, firing my pen.' John, a writer of verse, who is forever vowing to make us immortal through his prose, kisses my hand. 'I will inscribe your name in gold.'

'Vera, I must have you tonight.' Sal, a boxer with his nose spread across his face like jam, tries to push them both out of the way.

He says this to me most nights. As they speak, their fingers roam my breasts; they are savages. It is a fine mix for me. I like the poet and the savage. I am one too. I tell them this and they say yes, yes, mouths mumbling agreement. My father looks on, sucking down his cigarette.

'Let the girl breathe,' he says.

I sit down at his table.

'How is my little Venus flytrap?'

'Starving.' I pull his plate of spaghetti towards me. 'Daddy, I have written another poem. This one is about a woman broken by love.'

'Ah, an immortal theme.'

I read my poem to him. '...*Their skulls smooth like mine crack, in time to the splitting of my whalebone heart.*'

He tells me I am a great poet. He tells the men who try and perch on our table, 'My daughter, you know, is a great poetess.'

Their eyes glaze. I am honey, I am meat, I am all rump. I am not a poet. They see my lips move, but they hear nothing.

I say to Daddy, 'I must trap my little flies, for how else will I get them to stick to me, to listen to me?'

He is sympathetic, but even he, at times, only watches my lips move.

Jack is at my elbow. 'Vera, love, we must away before we are pumpkins and miss the fun!'

'I'll see you at the ball, Daddy.'

I lean down and give him a kiss. He is already so fermented, he is writing rhymes in beer on the tabletop. '*A woman's skin is like whisky...or gin...*'

'No, no, Venus, come sit on my lap. Don't desert poor Frankie.' Bald Frank, with his pince-nez dripping from his nose, is slapping his thigh.

'But Frankie, darling, I must change for the ball tonight. Jack and I sought only inspiration of a spiritual nature to aid our metamorphosis, and I believe we have had quite enough spirits.'

'Metamorpho, metamorphy what? Just one tiny drink with poor Frankie?'

Frank buys us a round of port. We toss it back and here it blurs, as drink tends to worry the edges of memory and time slops over itself. I was a mermaid that night. I saw a sketch of myself, my breasts bare, in the eyes of the illustrator at least, and I remember my legs in the green scaled cloth I had painted for the ball, with long slits down the sides so I could dance...That's it, dancing...the foxtrot, knees twisting, the streamers...such a crowd...We walk into the Town Hall and it is gay, so gay, and the colours: orange, black, purple all smashed together! Faces, too, pirates and cherubs, Caesars, Pierrots and a whole row of tin soldiers fall down dead; they are shot...bang, bang, bang, and I am shooting them or pretending to and everyone is whooping and the band, '*where the fellers chew tobaccy and the women wicky-wacky-woo*', gets our ankles kicking and my body is lit up, swinging, swinging, swinging like a firecracker!

My head is spinning, the walls moving and the paper roses hanging from the ceiling are dancing too. All the people squeeze me and there is no air. I go down to the basement. I sit in shadow. I am breathing so hard and my head is swaying...It is good to sit still where nobody can see me...

Then I hear a voice. It crackles down my neck: 'I am the Sheikh of Araby. Your heart belongs to me.'

I turn thinking I'll see a man in a sheikh costume like Valentino...but instead a skeleton stands before me. His face is all hollows. He extends an arm lined with bones and pulls me up to dance with him.

'*I'm all broken up over you*,' he hums the tune in my ear as he presses me close and all I can see are bones till I am sure I am in the arms of death...and I am dancing with death and everything around grows soft and far away so there is only us. Time has gone. Then he buries his mouth in my hair and whispers.

'I know you, Perdita. You write beautiful poems. I know you are the poetess. You see beyond what others see. I know how you sing like a lark inside the darkness.'

He kisses me, so deeply I feel he can see me, past my painted face, my golden hair, my eyes, truly into me.

'You were born to bleed in ink. You have the heart of all the great artists and you are lost – yes? – my Perdita, on the shores of this cruel earth, when you are meant to fly, to be borne on the air.'

When I try to speak, to ask how he knows my poems, he kisses me again and I am lulled by his sweet tongue, full as it is with promises I have ached all my life to hear.

Then he is gone. My head is clear as razors. I am lifted on clouds of light. I shine like one of those electric bulbs and my lover, he has just pulled the switch. Only then I realise the basement is a riot. There are screaming whistles and policemen storming the stairs. The floor is flooded in beer. Someone has unstopped a keg. Knots of men are fighting. They look silly, like play things. And I am strapped to the wall. I can't move…Friends said they'd found me stone drunk with make-up smeared all over my face, my mermaid scales in rags. I didn't tell them. I didn't tell them about my skeleton man, but I kept him close to me, chanting his words like a keepsake, like a prayer…a lark inside the darkness. I wrote a poem about him, an ode to my dark lover.

*My lover steals kisses, he hangs them to dry, they swing in the wind, they never dry…he stole a kiss from me this night we danced, his hands on my breast, his teeth in my…*He had white teeth against the black, a smile conjuring pain, bliss and the longing one has to be truly known, truly loved. It was one of those moments when all motion halts, leaving a pure drop of lucidity.

I asked about everyone's costumes, who was there, what they wore. I was determined to find out his name. I would put a face to those bones…None had seen my skeleton man. Then one night we were at Theo's, eating pasta and downing legions of wine. There was Tom, Sal, John and Jack with his new girl, Dawn. He had hooked himself up to a girl with money, so he was buying us all drinks. Dawn liked to scribble a bit, play piano, and she came with a rich Daddy – that's about the most Jack knew.

'You like writing then, Dawn?'

I lean over to fill her glass. Dawn is afraid of me. I have seen her look at me like most women do. They see my legs in their short flapper dress, then my oval face painted like a china doll. From then on, they are guarded and look at me always from under their lids. If their man is around they wrap their arms around him like he is a schoolboy who mustn't be tempted by any sweets. Dawn is new, though. She has only just come out of the nest and is playing in dark corners for the first time. Dr Sigmund would probably say she was trying to get Daddy's attention. I thought she was trying to taste a little life.

'It's only a hobby.' She crosses her legs and throws a sideways glance at Jack.

'Have you been writing long?'

'Since I was a little girl, just silly things, really. I wouldn't call it writing. I don't know why I told Jack…I suppose because he writes in the newspaper and somehow we got talking…'

'Have you read her stuff, Jack?' I ask.

Dawn turns a shade of red not far off the colour of the wine we are drinking.

'What? Oh, what stuff?'

'Any of Dawn's writing.'

'That's just a hobby, isn't it, darling? Did you see that article I wrote on the new visionaries of Sydney, Vera? I put your father in there...'

'Put me where?'

Daddy walks in with an older man who has speckled hair at the temples matching his grey three-piece suit. There is a slick look to him, like a neat oiled engine. He walks like he owns every inch of board he struts on.

'This is Mr Alistair Stevens,' Daddy says. He turns to Mr Stevens. 'They are a warm tribe of cannibals, I assure you, Al.'

'Well, I know Jack here. How are you, young rascal? Drinking your wages, I see.' His voice is deep and drawling... familiar somehow.

'Pursuing the muse as always!' says Jack.

'I read your piece on the bush as the new mythical frontier. Very fine work.'

Mr Alistair Stevens...the editor of *Jones' Weekly*! A wave of heat sweeps through my body. My palms grow moist. Has he read the poems I submitted?

Daddy comes around the table and gives me a kiss. He has whisky on his breath. He slides onto the bench so he is nestled close to Dawn. 'Who is this pleasing sprite?'

Dawn blushes again. Mr Stevens comes around and seats himself next to me.

'That is my sprite, Mr Brandon,' Jack says with a wink.

'Ah well, if there are no free sprites we must have free spirits!'

A notion Jack is happy to oblige. As the tide of wine flows, the group becomes merrier. Even Mr Stevens seems to be easing into the swing of the night.

At last I deem the time ripe for asking about the poems I sent into the *Weekly*. 'Mr Stevens, have you had a chance to read any of the poems I sent you? They're signed Vera.'

Mr Stevens gives an odd smile, the corners of his mouth twisting. 'Ah yes, you are the poetess.' He picks up my hand and kisses it. His lips are thick, familiar against my skin. I see his teeth flash white. 'My dear lady, I am the Sheikh of Araby, your heart belongs to me.'

'The Sheikh of Araby...' I murmur. Was this my skeleton lover?

'Your poetry, my lady, is the stuff of nursery rhymes. It has no meter, no learning and is for the most part crass and ridiculous. I would quicker piss your poems in this mug and drink them than I would print them.'

'But you said...'

'And I would say it again for a fuck like that. Really, you should keep to what you do best. There are many ways to feed a man's soul and your arse is truly sumptuous, my Perdita. That is true art!'

The table breaks into laughter, Jack, Sal, Tom, John, saliva running into their glasses. Even Daddy is laughing. Only Dawn does not laugh. For a moment I hold her eyes before I make it outside to be sick in the gutter.

That night I went to the police station and told them all about the sly grog served at Theo's. Constable Joe Chuck came down and threw all the bastards out in the street. After that I didn't write so much. All my spitting words were useless. They just buzzed in my head till I danced crazed until well past sunrise. The memory of my skeleton man came to me when I was out on a night full of wine and I found myself on a table, kicking my legs up, bare feet stamping amidst broken glass and beer. My bone man came to be not only Mr Alistair Stevens, but a joke the whole of life had played on me. I would put an end to it. I would play with death, walking the edge of each smashed bottle, baiting the glass to cut me or the cigarettes to burn me or the men with their eyes pinned to my body to crush me with their need...

So where is Death now, when I have cast all aside to see him? He is keeping his lady waiting. Where are the roses, the sonnets, the sweet nothings? Shall we dance again, my skeleton man, one last time? What keeps you? Are your bones hung now in a mouldy cupboard? Have moths eaten out your spine, like the fish will do mine? Or are you a costume hired only for a night? Can you return yours?

Even when I was coughing up blood, there was a satisfaction to it, knowing Death was near. But maybe he has been held up by a lovelier lady who is not so desperate.

Maybe she teases him like I used to before I began doing the chasing. Amazing how much pain gets locked in one's body. All these waves cannot wash it away, not until I give it up just so, let my eyes drop and there, just there, so gentle... tossing me like a rag child on a string bob bob bobbing to a rag tune...

'*I'm all broken up over you...*'

The water tugs at me, a thousand hands taking me down inch by inch. Nipping at my skin, a wreath for my body.

I am an island continent with ocean along my edges. My skin is shrunk, wrinkling, puckered as an old woman's lips awaiting her final kiss. Soon I will be more water than matter. The fish nibble at my ears, soft like a lover's hands. Are the hands tugging his hands? Or are they the children of the sea coming to take this willing sacrifice home? Hardly virgin, but no matter I am sure…

The hands are tongues now, lapping, a hundred cats at a hundred bowls of milk, feasting at my shores. It is a welcome invasion! Come colonise me, vanquish all life. It was rich of Keats to claim on his headstone that he was only 'writ in water'. Keats, who had a headstone and all, thought fit to carp. What chance have I that someone will remember my flytrap mouth, my songs, my lines of rhyme? If anything some old man may caress himself and mutter about a girl with legs high as ladders he climbed…all the way to Venus. Will I rise again, naked on a shell, nymphs arching at my feet, mermaids trailed in my locks? I think not. I think I will die like I was never born…My dear Keats, this is how one writes in water.

Between the Chapters...

Sybylla and I are left floating in the sea, silence lapping around the space where Vera had been. It is too cold a lament for such a woman. Sybylla begins swimming back to shore.

'Do we let her go? Just like that?'

Sybylla turns, glancing back at the smooth surface of the sea, no break in the waves to show it had swallowed a woman whole.

'*Water, water everywhere and all the boards did shrink...Water, water everywhere nor any drop to drink.*' She licks the salt off her lips. 'Quickly,' she says, 'swim. The winds are coming.'

Sure enough, the surface of the sea is changing, waves moving faster as if sped along by an unforeseen hand. The air pushes harder against my face. In the distance, clouds gather. I begin to swim quick as I can. The shore grows further in the distance the more I swim. I see Sybylla ahead of me, then all at once she disappears. There is not a trace of her. As I start to panic she reappears, her dark head way out in front of me. She becomes a beacon. I fix my sights to her bobbing head. Then she disappears altogether.

The shore is a sliver on the horizon. I cannot get closer. My arms grow heavy.

Fear splays its frozen hands over my ribcage, moving rapidly down my stomach. It makes me drink water as I kick out with my legs. I have two useless paddles behind me, limp and boneless. The force of the wind sweeps me along. It twists me like a spinning top in the sea. There is no sign of Sybylla. The sheer expanse of the ocean, endless rolls of grey stretch out around me. As the rain comes pelting down, a tiredness falls upon me. My arms and legs hang like rope. I sway with the rhythmic swell of the water. It is a lullaby, the silence in the centre of a storm...ever so gently tossing me, a rag child on a string bob bob bobbing to a rag tune...*I'm all broken up over you*...No, I will not join Vera beneath the waves. I pull my body through the water. After an eternity, I reach the shore and drag myself out of the sea, collapsing among the shells and seaweed.

When I wake, the winds are gentle and the sky is calm. One would trust a sky like this with one's life. I would have once. Sybylla is curled up on the sand. Her olive skin is once again covered. She has dressed herself, stockings, heels and all. I watch her while she sleeps. She is ageless. There are no creases in her skin. Her lids fold like pods over her eyes. It is as if she were born new in that minute. She reminds me of Byron, my baby.

The night falls, spread with stars hanging from a half-moon. Byron was born under the sign of the bull. The only shapes I have ever been able to see in the stars are the saucepan and the Milky Way. Tonight, for the first time, I believe I can make out the horns of a bull, the bulk of its body and four legs descending into star-shod hoofs. I hope my baby will be like a bull. I hope she will be strong. I hope she will charge through anything. I hope she will never be lost at sea. What can you do to protect a baby? I feel so dwarfed out here with the horizon and sea as my bedposts. I can't keep her from the winds forever.

Sybylla is stirring now, murmuring in her sleep. What dreams could she have with a life already so surreal? Her eyes snap open. She stares back at me. I jump and catch my breath. She smiles at me. Sybylla has crept into my thoughts again. I can tell. She gets to her feet and starts collecting pieces of driftwood. I notice how much wood is lying around us.

'There must have been a shipwreck,' she says.

I think of Vera's poem; her body's a ship's broken hull... beached upon the rocks...all the sailors...must drown, their skulls smooth cracking in time to the splintering of whalebone...'What will they say about Vera?' I ask. 'Is she right? Was she only writ in water?'

Sybylla builds the wood into a pyramid and lights it with matches she pulls from a pocket. Needless to say, they are dry. For a long time she says nothing. We stare at the sparks throwing shards of light into the blackness. There is no sound other than the fire and the crashing of waves. She throws in another plank of wood. The flames crackle higher to swallow up the offering.

'She is remembered. Come, follow me.'

We walk down to the rocks. Hard sponges filled with pores, they sprawl around the entrance to the sea. Pools of black water collect in the cracks between them. Still as they seem, these rocks swarm with life: starfish, shells, crustaceans stuck to the walls with a tenacity envied by the unfettered seaweed. We climb over them until we reach a rock that has the largest pool hollowed deep in its centre. The pool is perfectly round. That is what is strange among all this broken, fractured stone. There is not one tremor in the hand that drew it. Sybylla draws me closer.

'Do not be afraid,' she says. 'We will see if she was writ in water.'

We kneel by the edge and she dips a finger into the pool. She begins to trace what look like letters onto the surface of the pool. She must be pressing lightly, as I can see the tension of the water. The surface does not break. It trembles as if troubled only by the legs of an insect. Beneath her hand, a luminous light begins to form.

'It is the algae,' she says.

I have never seen algae like this. Soon the pool is lit with an eerie green glow. At first I think it is my eyes, but the water is becoming clearer. Pictures are forming in the pool. There is a girl seated in a leather armchair. I recognise her. She has a turquoise disc around her neck. The journalist. She is even younger than when I met her. In a chair opposite her is a man. He is old, so old his skin is dried up and flaky as desiccated coconut. Grey stubbly hair lines his cheekbones and covers his chin. It is as if birth and death are sitting conversing with each other. Between them on a table a cassette tape spins.

'Do you remember the daughter of the great poet Christopher Brandon?' I hear her ask. 'Did you ever meet her when you lived in Sydney all those years ago?'

The man mumbles and coughs into his beard. 'I do remember her with that awful regret of increasing years. A pretty young thing like you wouldn't know that yet. She was another one of those women one could have but never did fuck. Ah...Vera...' His eyes wander off, over the girl's shoulder, as his memories grow more alive than the scene in front of him.

'Despite her careless amiability, she oppressed me as too luxuriously blonde, strong-minded for all her angelic smiles. That fabulous beautiful bitch. The queen of all bitches! Gutter Venus, that's what we called her.'

The girl shuffles her papers. The old man's swearing unnerves her. 'Why was that?' She asks.

'Well, she was a whore.' He laughs, his belly shaking beneath his brown shirt.

The tape clicks to a stop. There is a ripple through the water. The old man, the girl and the leather armchair fuse into a mass of colour. I see a shot of silver streak underneath the picture as it blurs. Sybylla shoots her hand into the water. She holds up a fish. It wriggles in her hand.

'Are you hungry?'

She does not wait for an answer. She climbs back over the rocks and down to the fire. When I get there, she is baking the fish on a stick over the embers. As the smell blows towards me with the wood smoke, I realise I am starving. She hands me a piece. It is the softest white flesh. I would swear it had been cooked in butter with lemon juice and a hint of lime. It is a blissful scene: the ocean backdrop, warm fire, night sky, good food. I would be happy if not for the depressing pit in my stomach.

'Is this all you tell? Gloomy stories with unhappy endings?'

Sybylla sucks a piece of fish off its skin. 'I do not write the stories. If they were all make-believe then I would not believe them. Then we could never hear them and the women would never tell them. All stories are true in their fashion.'

Sybylla speaks in riddles. 'We did enter through the yellow wallpaper, remember? That is where I found you wandering. It is not my fault if the pattern is so awful!' She starts to laugh at me. She stands up, gesturing with a fishbone as she quotes a line from *The Yellow Wallpaper*: ' "*The faint figure behind seemed to shake the pattern, just as if she wanted to get out.*" Do you want to get out?' She points to me and then raises her finger to the moon, over-exaggerating each movement like a tortured Shakespearean actor. ' "*At night in any kind of light, in twilight, candle light, lamplight, and worst of all by moonlight, it becomes bars! The outside pattern I mean, and the woman behind it is as plain as can be.*" '

She is making fun of herself, her shadow self, Sybil Jones who stands onstage.

Something in her laughter, in the way she is jumping around on the sand makes me nervous. The whites of her eyes shine in the light of the half-moon.

'Are you saying I'm stuck here?' My breath catches in my throat. 'There's only one way out? But I have to get home. I have a baby and a life...' I start to panic, that sensation of drowning, frozen hands over my ribcage. 'What about the windows?' There were all these windows in the room with the wallpaper, I remember.

'They are barred. You can't jump out of them.'

'What then?'

'The only way out is to pull off more wallpaper. It is the only way to get out of the pattern. We have to travel through it.'

'Let's do it, then. Where is it?'

61

Sybylla looks at me, eyes tender as if I am a child of five. 'To get out we have to peel it, strip it off piece by piece, story by story. We have to meet the women who are caught under it or there is no way for them to get out. Or us. That's what happens when you enter a story. You become it. They are not safe things, stories. They are not for bedtime with a hot cup of milk, like you've been told. They're dangerous. Don't forget you almost drowned.'

As if I could forget the force of the wind, the pull of the water.

Sybylla quotes *The Yellow Wallpaper* again but not with the overdone gestures or the laugh: '"*Sometimes I think there are a great many women behind and sometimes only one, and she crawls around fast, and her crawling shakes it all over.*" The next story is not far from here. Just a few years on when the Depression hits. Come, we can find her through the pool.'

We climb back over the rocks to the perfect circular pool. It is black and still as if nothing had happened here only a short while before. Sybylla bends down. She begins writing in the water. Again, I cannot make out what she is spelling. The algae begin to glow. A different picture forms. Instead of a chair, there is a classroom, old-fashioned by today's standards. No computers or projectors. There are rows of wooden desks with wooden seats attached to them by green metal rods. In front of a blackboard is a large desk. A woman is seated with papers in front of her. The papers are scrawled with children's writing, messy and unformed. She is writing on them with a red pen, marking them with ticks and crosses. Occasionally she scribbles a note in the margins.

At first there is nothing remarkable about this woman. She is mid-thirties, has a long face, pale with freckles, and brown hair tied in a bun. She wears a long tweed skirt and a grey blouse fastened with pearl buttons at the neck. She looks like the archetypal teacher. Then I notice she is watching someone. Another woman has entered the room. The teacher keeps glancing up at her in a secretive fashion. She wants to watch but she does not want to be seen...

Stella 1932

I watch the charwoman sliding between the desks, her duster raising clouds of chalk. I pretend to mark papers. She is bending down now, picking up a screwed-up piece of paper. I see her pop it in her apron pocket. Is that what she does, read the nasty notes the children scribble for entertainment?

'Edward B. Thomas, I see you there. What is that you have in your hand? Open your hand immediately...Ah, a note I see. Would you like to read it for the class?'

Edward is trembling; he has gone pale. 'I...I...I can't, Miss...please...'

'Come up here, Edward, face the class...If it was worth writing it must be worth us all hearing..."Miss James walks like a goose"...Like a goose? Edward, what do you mean walks like a goose? Can you demonstrate for us how one walks like a goose?'

Is that what she will read tonight, if she can read, that is? Something deplorable? Not even imaginative. And will she chuckle to think of me walking and watch as I come to class, laughing behind her hand? Perhaps. I break the lead of my pencil. Her head spins around to look at me. It is the first time she has raised her eyes to mine. Normally they are on the floor. Has she been taught never to look a white woman in the eye? I put my head back down as though nothing has happened. She waits a moment, watching as I sharpen the pencil. She has her back to me as I leave the room. As I exit I feel the room sigh, her sigh, as the chalk settles down and she is alone.

I can appreciate that. I know what it is like to always be watched, but the watching I am familiar with is of a different sort. I am watched with eyes depending on me for everything. Mother and Father have withered into little birds that gawp with empty mouths. It is not so much that they need me to do everything they ask. They could have domestic help, but I give them the one thing you can't pay for. I am a blood bond. I am a daughter. With this combination there is an extra debt, one that only grows with time, accruing interest with each passing year. The frailer they become the more I owe them, in a kind of recession of my own growth from child to grown-up. It is all unspoken. They do not say anything. They simply wait for me to pick up their napkins, feed them, play cards with them, help wash them. Any lapse on my part is reproached with that most awful of reproaches: a look, or a silence.

Tonight I am worn from my day but I rush to wash the chalk off my hands and make tea. I still have essays to mark and much writing to do after I make dinner, clean up and help Mother and Father prepare for bed. A slipper that goes missing, a sheet tucked tighter, a warm glass of milk. Sometimes I wonder if it is a game for Mother, her only sport for the day to test my patience. It may be my heartless imagining but I catch a glint in her eyes at times as if she were willing me to crack, to slam the slippers on the floor, to spill the glass of milk. She has the same look as the troubled children in my class who push and push. Is it relief they seek? Some end to the tension that keeps us moving in the same patterns day after day, puppets on strings growing tauter by the hour?

I bring the tray into the sitting room. The bone china cups rattle on their saucers as I set it down. My parents are seated in their armchairs. Mother is wrapped in her rose print shawl. Father is playing chess with himself, as he is wont to do for hours.

'Is that milk fresh, dear? Have you checked the milk?'

'Yes, it is quite fresh, Mother.'

'The tea tastes peculiar. Does it taste peculiar to you, George?'

'No, dear.'

'How were the children today, Stella?'

'Good. I was giving them a lesson on Napoleon and one of them, you know, Roger McCrob, the one I said had more freckles than you could imagine? He thought Napoleon was a horse his Father laid odds on.'

Mother titters. Father's shoulders heave in a single silent laugh. It is the most one ever extracts from him. We chat and I make them comfortable, bringing Father his tobacco, stoking the fire for Mother who is forever getting chills.

She squints her eyes in the firelight. 'Flora rang this morning. It took me ages to reach the telephone. You had already left, dear. She is coming over on Saturday, with all her brood. Won't that be lovely?'

'That will be delightful.'

Flora is my sister. She has a perfect pink husband and two wonderful pig-fingered children. They think I'm bitter, as if soured by sitting here alone without a man, pickled on the shelf. Flora seems happy but I am not convinced. There is something about the way she flutters her hands and a dullness in her eyes that wasn't always there, like rising damp leaving a dank odour over walls before you can actually see it. I suspect she too is petrifying in her own way.

I remember playing with Flora, so many games…yes… there in the cupboards hiding, but mostly in the garden with the ivy and the elms and the huge fig trees, playing games of hide and seek.

'Flora, are you there? Are you there?'

And I would hear her bubbly laugh. Flora could never stop herself laughing, and she would always give herself away. Bright eyes, and we were close then, very close.

What would happen if I called for her now? 'Flora, are you there? Flora, are you there?' Nothing, I expect. Not a hint of laughter, not a shake in the leaves. After I put my parents to bed I sit at my writing desk in my room. I have more papers to mark and then of course my writing. I pull out the children's essays on Captain Cook's landing. I asked them to describe the scene. There he is disembarking his boat with all the soldiers around him. In the background are the natives, spears in hand. Cook puts the British flag in the ground. Mavis Babcock, one of my youngest pupils, has everyone cheering, even the natives. I wonder if they would have cheered. I would not be jovial if someone came and planted a flag in my garden. But perhaps they did.

I should ask our charwoman at school. I have not spoken to her yet, just watched as she moves around the room, a grace about her…They are meant to be savages. She doesn't look like a savage…It's preposterous for a history teacher to know so little about the natives. I cannot even mark Mavis properly. I push the essays aside as a wave of fatigue comes over me.

It is eleven o'clock already but this is the only time I have for myself, so I cannot go to bed yet. There is a story to edit for *Home* magazine, and a historic account of Governor Bourke and the founding of Port Phillip. I have yet to polish the first draft for the publishers. Before I begin my editing, I have a treat I have been saving all evening, ever since I saw it sitting in the silver tray on the hall table. It is a letter from Nettie. I slice it open. The paper rustles in my hand like autumn leaves, warm and crisp. Her handwriting spreads neatly across the pages, a tide of swirls, and already I can see several exclamation marks. Nettie writes like she talks, always jumping in her voice as her thoughts run away with her…

> *Dear Stella,*
>
> *What a pleasure to find a scrap of time to write this letter – almost as good as a yarn with you! Congratulations on 'The Light of Day'! – the reviews have been exultant. I myself find your technique terribly brilliant and your portrayal of Lucinda so actual I became distressed myself at her entrapment. I know the book will have a fine run!*
>
> *I am in a jumble of housework, research and writing anything that will bring in the bread and allow Vance to write what I believe will be an Australian classic. My latest work was a page of advt of Peek F's biscuits at 5 pounds. My name will now be spattered forever around some biscuits that may not be dissimilar to cardboard. In any event, we are surviving, which in these times is a triumph, and the children have new shoes for school!*

You spoke in your last letter of your lack of confidence over your latest manuscript. I am well acquainted with this devil – a sort of stage fright – all daring becomes timid. I envy those like Kat and Dymphna who can put all criticism down to the spite or ignorance of the critic!

But we must soldier on and, my dear, you of all our talent, never need doubt your self! On that note, I met a young man, Mr. Fred Miller, at the last meeting of the Fellowship of Australian Writers committee. He was coming down to Melbourne and enquiring after local writers he could meet. I am afraid your name slipped out! I do hope it would not be a great imposition but rather boldly I have attached the details of his arrival hoping you might squeeze him in for tea. Do let me know.

I hope I may see you myself soon – it has been an eternity. If I give you notice of my next trip to Melbourne, might we have lunch?

Love,
Nettie

What a ray of hope Nettie is. I feel I have gulped a lungful of air. I place the letter in my butterfly-engraved box. It is already jammed with letters, not only from Nettie but Eleanor, Kat, Jean and my other far-flung friends who write their visions among the distractions of life. These notes hold my sanity together at times, the only wind of intellect and spirit to sweep through my days. More awake now, I take out my manuscript, the story for *Home* magazine, and look on it with a kinder eye.

The next morning as I cycle to school, the chill penetrates my wool stockings. The wheels spin beneath me and my skirt billows out. All the air is fragrant with life. As I chain up my bicycle and walk to the entrance, I remember the goose note and my ease falls away. I feel all the children are giggling more than any other morning, and I am sure as I walk past them that their gurgling peaks as they dart about like mice. Miss Greene strides towards me down the corridor. She always walks with such purpose. There is a rush about her, a whirlwind tied to her shoelaces that leaves you breathless in her wake. Her arms are loaded with books.

'Morning, Miss James, have you heard the latest in the papers? They're jumping out windows now. I've never seen the like. All our men are losing jobs faster than rats bailing a ship.'

'Yes, it's terrible!' The news in the paper has been shocking for a good while now.

'They're closing down Bennington's Butter Factory. My own brother's going to be in the soup kitchens soon, with six children to support. Can you believe it?'

'Does he have savings?'

'Sure, but this won't be over tomorrow. All of it will be eaten up in no time!'

The bell rings for the beginning of class. Whichever child is the bell monitor pounds the brass.

'The bell tolls,' says Miss Greene, eyebrows contracting in a knowing look as if doom is inevitable. Then she is gone, the whirlwind racing off.

As I walk into the classroom, the children clamber to their seats, slates and chalk at the ready. The day passes in that steady rhythm of chants that constitute our history, the dates matched with the names or event that made them stand out from any other day. The only difference to this day is how worn some of my students are looking. Their hair unshorn, their clothes frayed and undersized. The most unkempt ones have a hungry look in their eyes. I can see a mother struggling to squeeze her child into last year's shirt, a table not so well laden as it might once have been. I can see in my classroom the economic debacle that is this date, this time. For the latter part of the day, I teach the royal lineage up to Queen Victoria. The descriptions of their plumage and decadence are as incredible in this moment as a fairytale.

I linger behind after the children leave for the day, their plaits and jumping limbs bolting through the door. They are off to play by the creek, to evade the chores, to pester Old Joe at the confectionery shop. Sometimes their freedom leaves me breathless. I pick up the duster and move it in circles across the board. I take my time, watch the letters disappear, a day's work erased. There is King Henry VIII and each of his wives disappearing one by one – Catherine of Aragon, Anne Boleyn, Jane Seymour, Catherine Howard and the lucky Anne of Cleves and Katherine Parr who held onto their heads. Did any of it stick in the children's heads? All these royal dames in a century and a country so far from here and yet our Motherland.

I hear the charwoman's steps and the rattle of her mop and pail. I sit down at the desk and leaf through my books. I wait. It feels strange to break the silence between us. I am not sure how to do it. 'What is your name?' seems too abrupt, too peremptory, as if I am demanding something. At the same time, light conversation would hardly be fitting. She begins mopping the floors. At last I ask in the most friendly way I can think of, casually, with a grin as if we were on a tennis court, 'You know, I don't think we've ever been introduced. My name is Miss Stella James.'

Now that is all wrong. She looks up. I can see the confusion on her face. Am I addressing her? Am I mocking her? I do not know what she decides. She bends and begins mopping again. The silence stretches. I am not sure what to do with myself now. I start to flick through my papers. I almost miss hearing. She says the name given to her is Ruby.

Can a name be given? I cannot even say that it is a beautiful name if it is not her own. But I do not know what else to say. 'That's a beautiful name.'

She does not respond. She is looking more and more intent on thrusting her mop between the legs of the chairs.

I take a breath. 'Ruby, I teach our history to the students, and I wonder if you would know if your people cheered when they saw us coming? One little girl wrote this in her story about us landing here and I did not know if you were clapping or cheering when we came.'

She looks up then. Slowly she puts the mop down. She tells me that we looked like ghosts, the spirits of the dead coming home.

White ghosts? I feel cold suddenly. I had not thought of how our pale skin would look to the natives. What an unnerving thought…to be a ghost. 'Thank you, Ruby. Oh, I had not realised the time.'

Ruby stands still and observes my haste. This time it is her watching me.

When I arrive home, I do not feel myself at all. I make tea. I chat to Mother and Father. I am quieter than usual as I sew up a hole in the elbow of Father's jacket.

'Are you ill, dear?'

There is a lot of fuss as Mother, who lives a life of all sorts of aches and illnesses, draws on her own expertise to label my particular malady. It keeps her occupied for most of the night and she blooms with health at the excitement it provides. Father, however, is in a cantankerous mood. He tells Mother she is full of nonsense, that she is making up her infirmities. He complains about being in a house full of petulant females. Father had always been a taciturn man, but after he returned from the Great War he fell into black fits. He becomes enraged at a fly on the wall or a smudge of butter in the jam.

Now his rheumy eyes alight on me as he drags on his cigar. 'Stella, what happened to that man, what was his name, the one you brought home from school?'

'He was my professor, Father.'

'Did you scare him off with all your big words, your grand notions about yourself? Too good to do what the other girls did? Too grand to settle down?'

We have had this conversation many times before and always it is the same. He wears himself out after a while. 'Flora knows how to make a man happy. Got two fine boys now!'

'Yes, Father.'

I push the needle harder through the cloth. I clamp my tongue between my teeth and vow not to say a word. At times the effort of this is like damming a flood. If I were to break my silence, we would all be swept away.

'Don't know where you thought all your learning would get you. Soon you'll be one of these new girls that smoke like us men, hey? Think they're free as the wind, these newfangled women taking all the jobs away from the fellas. You should be home with babies, helping a good man like Gordon.' Father shakes his cigar at me. 'Depraved harlots, those girls. If I ever catch you smoking, I'll disown you quick as lightnin'. No daughter of mine, do you hear me?'

The needle rends a hole in the wool. I will have to unpick and start again. 'Yes, Father.'

Without any contest of wills, he tires and begins moving pieces around on the chessboard. When the time comes for bed, Mother is restless, as if the stirring of old wounds in the room had somehow filtered through her.

'Stella, I need my pills tonight. I can't sleep without them!' I fetch her pills.

'No, not those ones. The new ones the doctor prescribed. I told you earlier, the ones in the pink bottle!'

I bring her the new pills.

'Where's my water? I can't drink them without water, dear. I need a warm glass of milk too, not cold. That's it. Flora's coming tomorrow. That'll be lovely. You must prepare tea. Enough for everyone. Now help Father take off his boots. You see he can hardly bend down himself, Stella!' She throws me that reproachful look.

When at last I have put them to bed, I retire to my room. I have no vigour left in me to mark essays and certainly no strength to write a decent word.

Saturday morning and I am picking flowers for our luncheon as a table decoration. I snip the stems with my clippers. As I cut the stalks of the camellias, I am back in the strawberry patch where Flora and I used to be sent by Mother to pick the fruit. I can see the tiny seeds now gathered on the ripe fruit, sweet and sticky. Dirt and the hair of our cat, Gregor, clings to our hands. Flora has wandered a way off. The picking of each strawberry becomes a routine for the fingers and the mind starts to dwell on other things:

a ladybird that talks, a cloud that has turrets and a great drawbridge descending from the sky. I hear stomping in the grass behind me. I turn and see Flora. She has smashed a fistful of fruit into her mouth and its red juice runs in streams all down her white smock. She's pretending she's been shot. We were always playing at being shot like Uncle Harry was. I was her mate and the cabbages, the rake and even Gregor could transform into the enemy at any time.

'Save me, matey!' Flora tries to choke out between the strawberries in her teeth. She is half-laughing as she dies.

Car wheels grate over the gravel in the driveway. The camellia falls from my fingers, petals fanning out on the soil. Lord, they are here already. I hear Flora's voice in the driveway. It is highly polished. It has a sugar-coated casing.

'Yes, darling. Come on, children, Grandma's waiting.'

For years now I have heard that voice hold everything up, bright and gay. It leaves one uneasy in its consistency, as if waking to the same sunny morning every day. By the time I enter the sitting room, they have all bounded in and the house shrinks, as it is wont to do on these occasions. The two children, Bert and Andy, are running around, making our china rattle. Flora's husband, Gordon, is towering over Father, bellowing about the weather in his ear. Mother has Flora by the arm and is telling her how fine the boys are looking. I slide into the room, close to the wall, and wait for the commotion to subside.

'Ah, there you are, Stella. Quiet as a mouse as always.'

Gordon comes over to shake my hand, followed by Flora who gives me a quick embrace. Her cheek is soft with powder.

'Come say hello to Aunt Stella,' she chirps at the children.

They pause in their tumbling to eyeball me for a moment and then continue their pursuit of each other.

She shakes her head and once again that voice glides out, and I realise it is like glue covering all the cracks in the exchanges of polite society. 'Boys, they do have their own minds.'

Everyone seats themselves at our oak dining table and the conversation moves from the children and their grand achievements and how tall they are growing to the latest in the newspapers. It is at this point we nod and lower our voices. So many out of work now, so many on the dole queues and each day another tragic tale about a starving family or a widow left penniless with eight children to support, one child crippled by polio. There is a relief though in our voices – at least it isn't us. It is some stranger whose picture would never remain too long in our memories.

'How's business with you, Gordon? Things still trotting along?' Father asks.

Gordon works as a pharmacist so, unlike the men in the mines, on farms or in the factories, he is as yet out of reach of the worst of it. Mind you, one wouldn't think he was a pharmacist from his big hands and thick fingers, hardly the sort you would imagine measuring pills or labelling bottles.

'There's some talk of pay cuts, but that'll be it I'm sure.'

He coughs and there is a short silence. The sound of the children playing in the garden is loud in the background. Out the window I see them trample the daffodils.

'And how's the scribbling going, Stella?' Gordon grins at me, his voice overly cheery.

'I'm finishing off a book on Governor Bourke.'

'Well, how's that, isn't that amazing? What a clever girl you are!' I twitch in my seat. I can't help it.

'I saw your name in the paper the other day, what was that rag, Flora?'

'Australian Journal.'

'That's right, and they were saying what a grand lady novelist you were, something about…what was it called… *The Delightful Day…*was that it?'

My shoulders tense. *'The Light of Day.'*

I clean a thumbprint off the polished oak table. Father is staring out the window. Mother has her eyes down on the table. They are always embarrassed whenever my writing comes up, as if I am performing a graceless breach of etiquette. When I have a bad review, their faces positively sour, as if they too have been badly reviewed and their fears about my wasting time and bringing shame on the family name are justified. When a review is good, they look slightly perturbed but refrain from pretending I am invisible.

'So with all that scribbling, do you have no time for a fella then, Stella? Or is there one you've been hiding, hey?'

'I'm afraid not, Gordon.' I stand up from the table. 'I'll bring in the scones for tea, shall I?'

'I'll come help.' Flora follows me into the kitchen.

'You know Gordon doesn't mean any harm.' she says, 'He's just clumsy like that sometimes.'

'It's no matter.'

We fill the silver bowls with jam and cream. I reach over to pick up the butter knife. Flora grabs my arm.

'Do you ever hate him?' she asks. It is the first time in years I have heard her voice without its polish.

'Hate who? Gordon?'

'No, Father! For not letting you take up that scholarship at Oxford. I know there was only free passage for boys and not girls, but he could have afforded it. You would have had a whole different life, not stuck here. That Professor Hicks said you were the best he'd ever had and with all your writing...' Flora's voice trails off.

I had no idea she would have remembered that, let alone thought about it.

'No, I don't hate him.' I gently lift her hand from my arm. 'Though he is a thwarter in many ways, that's how he is. They all expected me to get married like you, so what a poor investment I was at the time. Anyway, I'm writing still, I'll always write.'

She smiles at me for an instant, eyes lit with the sun coming through the glass. She holds my hand tight. Then she picks up the silver jug and napkins. As I gather the warm scones together I can hear her calling to Andy and Bert.

'Come on, darlings, wash your hands, come on inside now.'

At the end of the day, the conversation is fading, the scones are crumbs on lips and around the floor of the children's chairs. The boys are out in the garden again shooting each other over the cabbage bed. Flora has spilt a dab of strawberry jam on her cream dress. I don't think she notices.

That night I am marking my latest round of essays when my red marking pen starts to drift in my hand, a life all its own. I pull out a blank sheet and begin writing. It is a new story or at least the seed of it. I can feel it growing there as if feeding on the ink. The more I write, the more it grows. A stream of red ink unfurls and each word brings up another word, the first provoking the next and I am sure it makes no sense. At the end of this red stream I am exhausted, but also there is that thrilling sensation of a new idea, a new world surfacing beneath my fingertips.

There are images there: a cave made out of ivy where Flora and I used to play, an orchard ripe with fruit, a bucket of water fallen on the floor so the water is gliding between my feet, wetting my toes. Perhaps this is a story about Flora and me. Yes, it is a story about us, the way it might have been had there been no children or husbands, Mothers or Fathers ever to invade our little cave. It is presumptuous of society to assume a woman would want all these things. Maybe we are enough in ourselves.

I start to write in earnest, imagining if Flora and I had our own flat. We would live together and there would be no distractions. I would come home from work and write and Flora could do whatever she pleased and there would be no calls on our time, no tobacco to fetch or washing to do. Perhaps this is it. I could write about two sisters, spinsters who are happy, maybe one even refuses an offer of marriage! Why would she leave her sister to care for someone else? It is all too pleasant!

The shape of this idea, neat with a twist, is ideal for a short story. The sisters have a cosy flat and a yellow canary. They have their daily life well set out. They tend the garden. They have breakfast on the balcony on fine days. They have their favourite walks. A suitor comes, in fine tweed with carnations…yes. A respectable widow. He woos the younger sister, with her delicate cheekbones and gentle manner. He believes himself a rescuer of this poor old maid. He will save her from her inconsequential life. The elder sister contemplates the loss of the other, thinking it inevitable. At the last minute, the younger sister announces she cannot marry her suitor as she is much too fond of her life or, as she puts it to her sister, 'their habits'.

I write for the best part of the night. The birds are starting to wake by the time I am done. I am tired but content too, as though I had feasted well.

The next day I am taking a turn around the school gardens at lunch hour when I see a trail of smoke rise from behind the gardening shed. I walk over ready to give a stern reprimand. As I turn the corner of the shed I see Ruby sitting on an upturned bucket. She has a roll-your-own hanging from her lips. She is in a reverie, staring at some point between the fencing and the hedge.

'Oh, I didn't mean to disturb you. I thought it was the children. Please excuse me.'

She looks up slowly, avoiding my eyes but taking in my white shoes and the butterfly pinned on my blouse. She blows out a stream of smoke. She doesn't seem startled in the least. It is me who is awkward as I step back away from the shed. At the last moment I find myself pausing on the spot. There is something about Ruby. She keeps appearing in my thoughts...her skin polished, her dark eyes that draw one so deep...pools of syrup...They say they are a dying race, these blacks, the last of a primitive breed. She is a woman, though, just like me and Flora...and those eyes are not vacuous... Rather, they are sad, I think, and haunting...I see for a moment the ship of ghosts her people saw. I turn back.

'Where are you from, Ruby?'

She tells me she comes from the north where there is a training home for Aboriginal girls. She was put in when she was five. A man came around and told her family she was not being cared for and needed teaching. All she was taught was to scrub floors, mend clothes, iron and cook. She speaks with no emotion, like she is telling someone else's story, a litany of facts.

At one point her voice breaks from its monotone and she seems to forget I am there. She stares off again between the fencing and the hedge. She talks about scraps of memory, stories told around fires as damper cooked in the ashes. Stories danced and sung of snakes, emus, men and women changed to animals, creatures so alive she never knew whether she was hearing her aunty's voice or had slipped into dreams.

Ruby jolts herself upright on the bucket. She has forgotten I was there. Her eyes dart to the ground and her face closes up. She stamps her cigarette out on the ground. At that moment I hear footsteps on the lawn behind us. Miss Greene pokes her head around the corner of the shed.

'Oh, it's you, Miss James. I saw smoke before and thought it must be the children. I didn't realise you smoke…' Her voice rises in a question. 'Ladies are becoming so liberated these days, I suppose.'

Then she sees Ruby who has stood up, head down, fingers twisting behind her back.

'Ah…' She steps back in distaste as her eyebrows arch. She looks ugly in that instant and I wish she had not intruded on us. I want to apologise to Ruby for Miss Greene's ill manners. Instead I stand there waiting.

'Are you all right here, Miss James?' Miss Greene asks.

'I am quite fine, we were just conversing about…' I turn my head back to Ruby but she has gone, bolting off across the lawn.

'You don't want anything to do with those blacks.' Miss Greene sucks in her cheeks so the bones are jutting out on her face. 'They're not like us, you know. Are you coming?'

She walks back towards the classrooms. I stand a moment longer. I look in the direction Ruby fled. There she is...a small shape in the distance, flying across the grass.

That night I feel the seeds of another story growing, a story about a native girl. I see her standing there, holding an iron down on a white sheet. Perhaps she is a maid...working for two sisters. But there is conflict, a brother? Perhaps it is a love story, one that breaks all convention. Pressure rising to the point of release. Desire clamped down between the iron and the sheet...A native girl...the white brother...Her black skin, the call of the earth, the heart of this ancient land...her eyes drawing him in until...I am not sure yet. The ship of ghosts...a death...perhaps a fire.

I start writing. I have not written anything of this nature before. I have not tried a love story, and nothing as elemental as this. The drama of it enthrals me. I feel it has the form of a novel. And there is Ruby. It is her face I see as I begin to sketch my character of the maid, a native girl in a starched uniform. I will draw her as an emotional and loving human being. Not like anyone has written about the Aborigines before.

I see her now. Her face is lit by flames. That's it...she is stoking a fire. It is a cold dawn. There is a fog that mists all the glass panels. She can see her breath in the air, a balloon of white ice. Upstairs she hears the elder sister stirring, the sound of the coverlet hitting the bedroom floor. She goes to open the curtains. The birds are waking. I hear magpies from our own garden. It is dawn here too.

The following afternoon, I wait after the last class. I wait for the sound of Ruby's mop rattling against her bucket. I wait for her to walk in that way she does as if she were invisible, eyes to the ground, wrapped inside herself. I am not sure what I am waiting for exactly. Should I apologise for Miss Greene yesterday? Maybe I will ask her why she pockets notes she finds on the classroom floor. Does she read them? Can she read? Maybe they taught her the alphabet at that home in Cootamundra…Could she be teaching herself? Is that why she takes the notes? Maybe I could teach her…A…B…C…D.

I hear the sound of a broom being swept up the hall, the clatter of a tin pail.

Through the door comes a man. He is unshaven, wearing a sunken grey hat.

'Where's the girl?' I ask. 'Where's Ruby?'

'Don't know no Ruby, Miss,' he scratches his head 'Just got this job.'

'She was the charwoman here, a native girl.'

'Well, shouldn't be no jobs for girls, not with us fellas out of work. I got a wife and kids to feed. And a black, ya say? They're a crazy mob anyway, shouldn't be giving them no jobs. They must 'ave given 'er the boot!' He slides his rag over a few desks, gives the floor a cursory sweep and leaves.

I do not realise how long I am sitting there until I catch sight of the clock. It is quarter to five and I have forgotten all about Nettie's friend Mr Miller. His train is arriving in six minutes. I pack my books into my satchel. I ride my bicycle to the station. I am late and Mr Miller is already standing on the platform. I know it is him by the book he is holding in his hand. It is one of mine. Perhaps he means to flatter me. His shoulders are broad in his grey suit. His dark hair is swept over his brow in a Byronic style.

'Mr Miller?' I am not what he expected. A trifle older and greyer perhaps, drabber than he was hoping.

'Miss James, what a pleasure to meet you! I have a book of yours here.'

'So I see,' I indicate the volume he is holding.

'Yes, yes indeed.' He smiles like a raffish boy. He knows how to charm ladies. 'It was good of Nettie to write to you.'

'I hope you had a comfortable journey from Sydney?'

'Yes, it was pleasant enough.' As we walk through town to my house, our talk turns naturally to writing.

'I am working on a most daring novel. It is a commentary on the Battle of the Somme from a cosmopolitan outlook. It is told, you see, through the eyes of worldly, war-worn soldiers; battle horses, really. I'm hoping it may win the Christopher Brandon Literary Award.' For most of the journey, he tells me in detail about his characters, the action of the plot and so forth. Eventually he turns to me.

'And you?' he asks.

'My next book will be a love story, actually.'

By the polite smile on his face I can tell he expected this of a woman. At the same time he is wondering how a spinster like me can know anything about love or desire. 'Ah yes, how charming. You lady novelists adore romances,' he nods at me. 'Is it a drawing room escapade?'

'It is a story of love between a native girl and a white man.'

'Oh!' his chin falls. 'Well I…I didn't…What? An Aborigine?'

'Yes.'

'Why? What would you want to write about the blacks for? And with one of us?' Mr Miller's face reminds me of Miss Greene's the other day behind the garden shed.

'Why wouldn't I?'

'Well I…I don't know that you'll get that in print!'

For the rest of the journey home, Mr Miller is mostly silent. I tell him about the two sisters and the setting for the book. He nods again politely from time to time. When we reach the house, Father greets us with a show of surprise.

'Ah, a young man. They are a rare species around here, my boy!'

I feel the dam of my tongue pressing hard on the roof of my mouth. 'Please don't mind my father, Mr Miller,' I say, at which point Mother appears and makes such a fuss of him, I can barely contain myself. 'I shall make us tea.'

When I return with my tray of cups and saucers, I seat myself opposite Mr Miller. I watch him carefully. I can tell as he sweeps his eyes over the wallpaper, over Mother's face, over Father's bald head and tattered slippers, over me with my hands folded over my knees, that we all look faded to him. I pour us tea, placing a shortbread on each saucer.

'Stella, where's my tobacco?'

I fetch Father's tobacco from the box on the mantle. Mr Miller draws out a cigarette case and taps the tip of a cigarette on the embossed lid. I think of Ruby, her roll-your-own between her lips, sitting there on her upturned bucket, eyes fixed at some point between the present and the past.

'May I have one of those?' I ask Mr Miller.

'Lord, I had no idea you were one of those modern ladies,' Mr Miller exclaims.

I place a cigarette between my lips. I see the ink stains on my fingers, darkening my nails like bruises. Mother's face pales in horror.

'Stella, what do you think you're doing? You'll shock your father!'

Their faces recede, Father's cheeks red, Mother's eyes wide. Through the smoke, I see Flora hiding inside the ivy, laughing. I see Ruby running across the oval, free as the wind. And I want to run, tear across this dry land to the sea and get back on the ghost ship that brought us here. I want to travel far away, to London or New York or Paris, where for all the smog of the city I might breathe. I inhale on the cigarette and take a sip of tea.

Between the Chapters...

Smoke clouds the water. Behind the ghostly curls of her cigarette, Stella fades from the surface of the pool. There is no shake of a fish to excite the water. She retreats quietly as the algae dim from green to black. I want to put my hand in and lift her out. Or perhaps I could jump in and we would drink tea together?

I knew a lady who read tea leaves. She was a friend of my mother. I remember her long red nails tapping against the side of the china cup. I remember the way she swirled the tea and 'aahed' as if my fate was sealed. There was no more for me to do or wonder about. It had been written in the Earl Grey tea. She became magical, this lady. Possessed of a sight beyond mine.

As a child I was in awe of her. I kept checking her face to make sure she was telling me everything, the whole truth. At times she would breathe in sharply and lower her eyelids. I would ask her what it was but she would say nothing. I was convinced I was about to die and she didn't have the nerve to tell me. I even wrote a will out once after her visit. Mum came in to find me dividing all my toys. I said I would give her my favourite pony, 'Bloom', complete with brush and saddle. Mum said she would be honoured to have my little plastic pony but that I wasn't going to die.

After that, when the lady came around, she never read my tea leaves. I can still remember her and Mum sitting in the kitchen, though, cups of tea in hand. Mum would be looking at her with a little of the awe that I had. The lady would swirl Mum's tea around. When she gave that secret look, I could tell Mum was nervous. Mum would light up a cigarette and hold her breath.

One time they had a fight. It must have been about the tea leaves. The lady didn't come around for many years, not until I turned sixteen. On my sixteenth birthday, she arrived at the house. Mum hugged her and they cried. When all my friends had gone home and the lounge room was littered with cake and paper plates, she took me into the kitchen. She told me to make us a cup of tea. As the kettle boiled, I remember I was so nervous I kept biting my nails. Her nails were still perfect, like the talons of a dragon.

That night she told me I would marry a fine young man. He would have black hair and a crooked front tooth. This was a very fortuitous sign. He would be kind and we would have many healthy children. That was it, my fate was sealed.

Sometimes when I drink tea now, I look hard at the bottom of the cup. I wonder if the leaves can change. If you mix them around with your finger, would they make another pattern? Perhaps I could tell Stella about the tea leaves. I would help her stick her finger in the cup and mix hers around so maybe everything was not so set, so inevitable.

Her fate might open wide: a boat passage to France, a house of her own. We could change the way everything played itself out for Flora and Ruby. Surely there was a way, another story to be told...I lean in towards the pool. Sybylla grabs my hand.

'You must never touch the water,' she warns. 'Remember, stories are alive. They are dangerous. You do not want to get more embroiled than you already are. Even I may not be able to save you.'

The dawn is coming as we make our way back to the dying embers of our fire. The clouds move quickly overhead. I hope there is not another storm brewing. I can smell sulfur and dust.

'This is no storm,' says Sybylla. 'We are passing through a dark time. The Depression is over but the war has started. Nothing can touch us here. It is beyond the horizon.'

She kicks sand over the last glowing ashes and heads away from the sea. She walks towards a track I had not noticed before. It is cut into the mounds of tea-tree that line the beach. The branches, tortured by the ocean winds, have moulded themselves into the strangest forms. They sprout out and curve around as if arms and legs, even bodies were entangled in their trunks. As we enter the tunnel of trees, shadows fall upon us.

'You say I only tell gloomy stories. Stella's time was better, yes? Many women were telling stories. They printed many books, more than ever before, even if they are lost to us now.'

But what about Ruby? What did she do without a job? Did she ever see her family? Stella never really saw Ruby. She only saw Ruby as a white woman would see her at that time. It is hard knowing there are women behind this wallpaper who never get near the outside pattern. Trapped always underneath, behind the shapes of other women even, who keep them locked in. These women are wallpapered over again and again. In time, they are stuck behind layers of glue, paste and faded prints. Who ever heard Ruby's story?

Sybylla turns with that smile she has when she creeps into my thoughts. She places her hands behind her back so I cannot see them. 'Choose one,' she says.

I tap her shoulder. As she draws her right hand out, I see she is holding a book. It is bright red and 'Auntie Ruby' is printed across it in silver lettering.

'See who wrote it?'

There are two names for the authors, one is Wenonah Jones and the other is Ruby Jackson. Is this Ruby? I open the book to see when it was first published. It reads only seven years ago.

'But Ruby lived in the twenties, how could she —?'

'Wenonah is Ruby's daughter. Ruby did return home and her story is told here, with her daughter.'

I clutch the book tightly. Even those stuck far behind the most awful patterns can get out! The silver title gleams with a magical light in the shadows of the trees. Ruby's name stands out on the cover, an affirmation and challenge to all who would render her invisible. As I hold the book, its warmth radiates into my hands. I feel the real power of stories and what storytellers like Wenonah and Ruby can do. They resurrect the dead, give voice to the silenced, remember the forgotten. No wonder they are such dangerous things. I walk faster beside Sybylla. For the first time, she takes my hand.

We have been walking a while when Sybylla turns sharply to the left and walks into the bushes. I follow quickly, trusting she knows where she is going. Sure enough, instead of spikes and thorns, the bushes melt away. I hear them rustle as they close behind us. When I look back the trees have disappeared altogether. I find we are walking up a concrete driveway. We are approaching a suburban-looking house with red brick, a patio, and a lawn with hedges so trim they look like blocks of Lego.

'Shall we have some dinner?' says Sybylla.

But she does not walk up to the front door. She sidles around the side of the house, walking right along the wall, in the garden beds. She crouches down and peeps in a window. I creep beside her and take a furtive look. There are four people, two men and two women, sitting down for dinner. The whole scene is just like a 1950s movie set, with chintz curtains, peach carpet and a laminex table with vinyl chairs. One woman is wearing a green checked cotton dress. The other is in a floral print. The men are in suits with big collars and broad ties.

The one that catches my attention is the woman in the green checks. She is not quite in the conversation. She is listening to something. It must be the music. They are playing a classical record. It is not the music one would expect at a dinner party. It is sombre, almost funereal. The woman in the green checks looks lost in it, as if it has caught her and she is not sure how she is going to get out. I turn to Sybylla. She has her eyes fixed on the woman in the green checks as well. There is a strange look on her face. Her eyes are glazed and even the shape of her chin and the slope of her cheekbones seem different. There is a blackness around her lashes and her lips are redder, as though she has bitten them hard. I have not seen Sybylla ever look like this. It is as if someone else were crouching there beside me. I hear her whisper, more to herself than me.

'Ah, there's Eve. She's ready. Would she notice if I were the pin that burst her bubble?'

Eve 1954

She came to me from a piece of music, Tchaikovsky's 6th Symphony. It is playing in the background while we are dining at the Randalls'. I am floating full of thought and air when I am landed by a stab of emotion, a prick inside… the surfacing of something. It enters quick and sharp, and leaves me bleeding a while as the others sit and eat, pork fat dripping from their lips.

They do not notice. Not the Randalls nor my husband. I run my fork across the patterned china, tracing lilacs with the plum sauce. All the while the music rises, a mad storm twisting amid the chatter of bowls and glasses. It is a tempest and I see a woman there in the wind, howling. Her head is bent, her mouth open and her eyes black. Her make-up has run. Lipstick smears her cheeks. Her skirts are lifted, her thighs bare and wet. A baby lies on the ground at her feet. It does not move. The woman is stomping in grief or ecstasy or some emotion that cannot be contained in the walls of this house…with the pork and the pastel-pink walls and the lemon-iced sponge sitting on the buffet, ready to serve…

'Are you done, Eve?'

Valerie Randall is at my side.

'Yes, it was delicious. How did you make that plum sauce so sweet? Mine is always too tart.'

'It's just an extra half-pound of sugar. I know the recipes say just one, but plum is a bitter fruit and needs that little sweetener.'

Valerie steps away in a clutter of crockery and scraped plates. John and Richard sit discussing politics. I feel the pressure of decency to rise and retreat to the kitchen, allow the men to talk as we gather the dessertspoons and whip the cream. But I cannot move. I am pinned to my chair as the strain of violins delves deep into a rift as pregnant as a cloud, dark-trimmed and hanging low.

My woman is squatting now over the baby, her black wet hair dragging in the dirt. The child does not move. There is blood idling around its head. Has she killed it? The thought of such an act sends chills over my skin, a cold wind across the dark waters of a lake…and there is a lake behind her and in the far distance a house, small and ordered with a row of other houses. The woman raises her head then and smiles at me. As the music grows to thunder in the background, she rises to her feet and begins to sway, faster and faster until she is dancing. Bare feet in mud, hair swinging, she is laughing and crying and in that movement such abandon, such freedom, like a bird stretching up to flight…

Valerie comes back from the kitchen, balancing saucers and spoons with the bowl of whipped cream. Richard casts me a look across the table, eyebrows raised.

'Oh, Valerie, I am sorry! I became quite distracted by the music. Let me give you a hand there.'

'This heavy classical stuff? It's so morbid, isn't it? John loves it. It makes him feel intellectual. Isn't that it, John? But why you must inflict it on our guests! Go and put on some Crosby, darling.'

The moment John lifts the needle, my mad woman in her storm ceases to dance. Gradually, as the lemon-iced sponge is served and the neat tunes of Crosby's 'Where the Blue of the Night' quell Tchaikovsky's symphony, she fades into the chintz lounge and apricot blinds.

'Eve, I saw some lovely slacks in *Australian Monthly*. They're nipped in at the waist with a tapered leg line. John's adamant he prefers me in a skirt, so I'll have to win him over...'

'I do love that dress you're wearing.'

'Thank you! The lady in the shop told me it was "slenderising", and I do need all the help I can get after two children. I'm rather naughty having this cream tonight!'

There is a short silence. I can't think of any small thing to fill it. Something we have in common, perhaps...We concentrate hard upon spooning the cream onto saucers. Maybe I should ask about the children?

'Are you writing still, Eve?'

'Oh, just dribs and drabs. With Todd to look after and another on the way, there won't be much chance.'

We glance conspiratorially at the large mound stretching out the green checks of my cotton dress.

'Well, I know it's hard with the little ones, but I hope you do keep on. I did very much enjoy your books and that play you did for ABC radio. Both John and I were in stitches!'

'It's been a while since then. With the war...it just felt too big, too tragic to write my nonsense. What did it matter with all that mess, bombs killing our young men, my brother Reg and Joe, Richard, John out there in the mud. Silly to think I had anything to say!'

'Every little bit counts, and it's been years since then. Just think of us bored housewives if you need a cause. Anything to take our minds off all this hubbub.' She nods her head at John and Richard. Richard is swinging his dessert fork in John's face.

'You can't ban a political party in Australia, not even Menzies. It's just not democracy!'

'There is no democracy,' John protests. 'Just subtle dictatorship!'

'It's strange, isn't it?' I look at Valerie. 'Sometimes I think having a baby now is foolish, what with the A-bomb and all. It's like the war never really ended. The danger never went away, it just grew quieter.'

'I wouldn't call these two quiet! Let's not get gloomy about it. Imagine if we had to build shelters, like the Yanks do. Then you could come over and play bridge with us underground!' Valerie laughs.

She has a delicious laugh, soothing on the nerves like a balm. I try to join in but I sound like a stick striking tin. That night as I lie beside Richard, the solid form of his body comforts me. It lies between me and the world, immovable... insurmountable.

I wake right on five o'clock. I have not risen so early for years. Up at five to do a couple of hours' writing before breakfast, I would sit at the kitchen table and feel the frost from the hills bite my fingers, so I had to rub hard to make them work while the heat from the oven filled the room.

This morning, I soak in the familiar sensations of dim light carving its way through the curtains, the cool stillness of dawn. I woke from a dream and slowly it comes back to me. The strange character, the barefoot woman I imagined last night had been in it, dancing again to music…I cannot remember more…eyes darkly ringed, a hand opening and shutting, wet feet on gravel…With that old urge I thought had abandoned me, I rise out of bed, chasing the fragments of her face. *What is her name?* I ask as I pull on my robe and slippers, quiet so as not to wake Richard. *What would you call a woman like that? If she is a character, what shall I call her?*

'Judith.'

It is as if the name has been spoken aloud. I jump. Silly, I think, silly to frighten yourself. All the same, the morning has an eerie magic to it, like a doorway to another world. That is why I've always liked writing early. Though of course it becomes a necessity when one has to accommodate a family and all that housework. There was no chance then to slip through gateways. I pull out the notebook stored in the kitchen drawer. I sit facing it: my old friend, my old foe. *Let me meet her, then*, I whisper under my breath as the leaves of the wattle outside stroke the glass.

She is sitting on a kitchen stool in a kitchen much like mine. There is the Mixmaster on the bench, the blender, and the frying pan ready to go on the stove. She appears dressed as a mockery of a housewife, an apron on and a handkerchief around her head all askew. Pieces of her dark hair fly out of a net around her sharp-boned face. She is waving a feather duster at me and raving, talking fast and fervently, with a shiny look to her eyes like she has a fever.

'So, everything's all right as long as the couch is all right, as long as it does not fall open and gaping and let its cover drop, showing all the gaps, the crumbs, the tattered edging, 'cause I'm the only one who sees that, who notices the grime and grease slipping from floors and walls into my skin till I have to scrub and scrub to feel clean, whole, good again. My house is a whole creaking mess mirroring the untidy nest of my life. It looks fine to the stranger, well cared for, even, but there are holes everywhere and that's what I hide with cushions, the porcelain clock, the bright smile. But they don't know these holes, they don't know when they walk into my kitchen they are skating on thin ice. Any moment it might swallow them whole, any moment the grease might tip the world upside down with the weight of its filth. There are products everywhere to clean with. This dirt is a disease, an invasion and there are germ-killers everywhere. I buy them by the trolley full, every new gadget, every new stain remover and white brightener. The world is trying to get clean, sparkling bright and clean. The dirt of all the wars has made everyone as paranoid as me, and they dump it all in the magazines on us wives with their radiant floors, glimmering teeth, bad odour, bad breath, eliminate every telling sign of rot, of life. My house is a fortress under attack constantly from within, and the children and man, those I am meant to keep house for, are my enemies. With the lightest touch they spread disease as easily as a dog would defecate in the street. They are blind to my constant battle. They don't care. It's expected, for I have all these brains, this strong body for nothing but to keep their sheets taut, their table clean. My fantasy is to set it all on fire. That's it, leave the gas on and instead of fixing up the covers on my couch, I will grab the blue cloth and set it alight. All the germs go up in smoke and my world is as neat *and flat as a square of black earth. Eve, would you like a little bonfire for breakfast?'*

I am stunned by the outpouring of my pen. I have not written anything of this nature before. I sit for a long time watching Judith. She smiles back at me, lips barely moving. I hear movement in the house, the floor creaking, a rustle of sheets. I look at the clock. It is near on eight already and I have prepared nothing for breakfast. Richard will be up and dressing and Todd has probably been awake for a while. I race around the kitchen, frying up bacon, buttering toast, cracking eggs. I am like a machine that has malfunctioned.

Richard walks in, brow crinkled, mouth pursed. I have not been there to do his tie, is that it? Or did I forget to put out the right shirt last night? My mind thumbs through all the possibilities.

'Eve, there's a crease in the back of my jacket!' he turns around. There is a small crease in the fabric. 'What sort of doctor do you think people are expecting? One who looks like he slept in his clothes?'

'That won't take a minute dear, I'll just iron that out.'

'Isn't breakfast ready?'

'Almost.' I finish frying the eggs and dish them up.

Todd comes running in from his bedroom, yelping and jumping.

'Are you a puppy today, darling?' I run my hand through his curls. He yelps again and tries to lick up his breakfast.

'You can be a puppy, but you must eat like a little boy.'

I iron out the crease in Richard's jacket while they are eating, and dress Todd for school. Richard gives me the list of phone numbers of the cases he is visiting today so I can contact him at any time.

'Remember,' he says as he always does, 'don't leave the phone. Anybody might need me anytime. If you need something from the shops, have Brent's boy Toby fetch it.'

A kiss on the cheek and he is off. Todd tumbles out the door after him to catch the school bus. I turn back inside. The house settles into itself again. The peace is deceptive, though, for I have a mountain of things to do. The dirty breakfast dishes on the bench depress me. I think of Judith waving her feather duster. No point in dwelling on the dirt even if it does appear to spread as you clean. I can do the dishes later. I eat some scraps of toast and spend the morning doing the laundry, ironing, fixing the beds.

I am wiping the kitchen benches ready to do the dishes when I catch sight of my notebook, tucked under the newspaper. I must have hidden it when I was making breakfast. I sit down at the table and open it. Sure enough, there is Judith, kerchief crooked on her head. She is laughing at me, match in hand. She has left the gas on. With a flick of her wrist, she throws the match down and runs out the door. As I see smoke rise from Judith's house by the lake, I realise the phone has been ringing. Urgent, urgent...

'Always answer the phone, Eve, never leave the phone. It could be a life on the other end of that and your failure here could be murder!'

Richard's voice bangs in my head with the ringing of the phone. A doctor's wife, the task a doctor's wife must perform like a soldier, dutiful. Answer the phone.

'Never stray too far. Nothing, not your scribbling, your frocks, your flowers are more important than this phone.'

Richard had been by the phone when he laid down his law, slamming his hand on the receiver. I thought at the time how good and strong and practical he was. I was thrilled to hear the deep urgency in his voice. I had an important job now.

'Yes, Richard, of course, Richard.'

So many years ago that, and since then I jump whenever the phone rings and streak in from the garden or laundry or kitchen. Hands full of clothes, wet with suds, floured from baking, I would berate myself if it rang more than three times. Once I twisted my ankle on the step as I ran in, a spasm shooting up my leg as I dragged myself up the hall.

'Yes, Dr Barry's residence.'

Amazing how the voice can glide, smooth over any feeling, any pain. When I had tried to write, the ringing would cut straight into my head and all my words drain from my pen. When I sat back down, the paper appeared a vast void I could not imagine filling now with people flimsy as shadows. There was always a moment of grief, as I never knew what I had lost. But still it could have been a life on the end of that phone and the fact that it was only Mrs Jeffries with her boils was no reason to think more of my words than was due to them. After all, what I imagined may have been splendid could easily have been banal, or as one critic said, 'Empty of all thought.'

Was that it? Or no, it was more definite than that.

'Mrs Barry,' they had said, 'is obviously not much of a thinker.'

In all my writing time, though, small as it was, hoarded from hours allotted to housework, childcare and meals, had the phone rung and I had not even heard it? I grip the side of the table and leap to my feet. How long has it been ringing? I run to the phone. As I pick it up, I hear the click at the other end. Richards's words thunder in my mind: 'Someone may be dying...in severe pain...needing help...tantamount to murder!' My throat tightens. I cannot breathe, just short breaths, gasping as a wave of panic rises from my stomach to a knot in my chest. It could have been Mrs Jeffries, I tell myself, just Mrs Jeffries, or the Macys' child who sneezed once and she would call Richard. Richard...what if he finds out? Whoever it was would be sure to tell him.

'I rang, Doctor, but it was most strange; there was no answer. Where's that wife of yours got to?'

Or if it was a crash, someone lying on the road waiting...I pace back and forth, twisting my hands, knotting my fingers as I wait, praying for it to ring again. Nothing, just silence growing fat and heavy. Finally I walk back to the kitchen table. My notebook is spread open, the last line winks up at me.

'Eve, would you like a little bonfire for breakfast?'

She even used my name. I mean, *I* even used my name. Is that sane, to write a character that addresses you in such a manner?

I sit back down at the table.

'No, Judith,' I write, 'I would not like a bonfire for breakfast.'

'Oh, surely just a small one for starters; you could begin right here in the kitchen. Or if fire's not your thing, why not smash a few of those plates? You know you don't want to wash them. All that dirt keeps coming back, breeding. Haven't you thought that, Eve? The dirty plates are breeding!' She is laughing at me.

'With a more destructive streak in you, Eve, you'd have more time to spend with me. But you don't like me much, do you? So

what about some poetry instead? You'd have more time to spin your lyrical lines. How long has it been, Eve? Remember when you were a budding girl, you said you would write such a sky-splitting poem? Sky-splitting, no less! The young should be careful what they say. It comes back to haunt you, all those promises you make, all those wild ambitions gone hungry. They'll get you in the end. The ground goes cold beneath your feet and your own steps pursue you as you walk, beating out empty days of an empty life!'

I pause, my pen wavering above the page. I have not thought of my poetry in years.

'What melodrama! I am quite content,' I write back. 'The poetry...well, you know with Todd and Richard and life... you grow up.'

'You grow old. You do not grow up. Now I see you are tied to quite a different line. A phone cord round your neck, hey? Why don't you take the phone off the hook, let us talk in peace?'

With a jolt I remember the unanswered call. 'Unthinkable!'

'Cut the line. Or do you enjoy the power, a life in your hands? You as the omnipotent link? Very necessary, aren't you, Mrs Barry? But you missed a call, didn't you? Are you a murderess now? I shan't ask how that makes you feel. I have a fair idea.'

I see her then vivid as I did when the strains of Tchaikovsky's symphony conjured her up. She is standing over that form on the ground, her hands together in front of her, nun-like, palms pressed. She raises her eyes. They are dark and slippery, the flash of an eel's coat. Then she murmurs, almost chanting, *'Henbane, bryony, monkshood, rue, hiera picra, holy bitter, henbane, bryony, monkshood, rue, hiera picra, holy bitter, holy bitter, holy bitter, holy bitter, holy bitter, holy bitter...'*

Henbane, bryony...poisons...and holy bitter...what does that mean? It sounds more a curse than a plant. It has come out of my head so I must know it...What a strange apparition to have, not decent at all. What sort of character is this? What sort of story could come from this? Todd's feet shuffle up the path. What relief! I run to the door and swing it open. There he is, his face as sweet and normal as ever. I throw my arms around him and squeeze him until he squeals.

'Mummy, you're hurting me.' He wriggles out of my arms. 'Sorry, darling, I just missed you terribly. How was school?'

'Good, Miss Lambert said I was a top speller and she let me write on the board.'

'What did you write?'

'Apple, orange and banana, 'cept I had trouble with banana cause there's too many 'n's.'

When he says 'n's' he screws up his face and his tongue sticks out between his teeth. I have to stop myself grabbing him again.

'Well done, darling. Are you hungry?'

'Starving.'

I make Todd a ham sandwich. Then we whip up a mock-cream filling for the American-style sponge I baked the day before. He pretends the whisk is a propeller on a bomber as he beats the butter and sugar. We cut out leaves and flowers from pastry to place on top of a steak and kidney pie. When Richard comes home he makes a fuss of our decorations. Todd sticks his chest out and grins.

'I did it all, Daddy. I did!'

'That's great, son, but I think you're spending too much time with Mother in the kitchen. Where's your cricket bat?'

Todd pulls his chest back in.

We are about to eat when Richard asks me the question I have been dreading. 'Did you have many calls today, darling?'

'I call you whenever I have a patient phone, Richard. Quieter than usual today.'

He studies the plate in front of him.

I hold my breath and try to look as natural as possible.

'Did you know Mrs Johnson's still got that earache. For the blazes of me I can't work out what's wrong with her. I think she may be making it up.'

'Maybe she likes having you around, darling.' I breathe a sigh of relief.

'Well, she keeps saying I'm a Red because of that article I wrote on state health care, but she says she *has* to trust me as I'm a doctor.'

'Well, that's reassuring.'

We laugh and I dish him up a second serve of pie.

I wait till that night in bed to ask him about holy bitter. I say it casually as if I were asking the weather forecast.

'Darling, what's holy bitter? It's a herb, isn't it?'

Richard's face goes white. He stares at me, 'Why would you ask about that?'

'It just popped into my mind. I think I heard of it in school or something.'

'Eve, it's an abortifacient. It's for abortions!'

'Oh, heavens, however did I hear of that?' I giggle.

Richard does not stop staring at me. 'Eve, you...'

'Don't worry, darling. It was just a silly thing. I don't know how it popped up.' I chat on for a while and rub his shoulders until he falls asleep.

I wake at five again the next morning. This time the cold bites into my bones and it is not so charming or magical. Instead the light is unfocused. How can I see clearly in this light? How can anything be proper or ordinary when all one can see is the odd angles of shapes? I rise out of bed. I feel I am summoned back to the page and like a servant I move without thought or question. Richard lies still, snoring. I glance at his large bulk for a moment. It is as if I am fleeing the marital bed for some strange liaison, an escapade, an illicit affair.

'Judith, Judith,' the pulsing of her name through the stillness and then pounding in my head, 'holy bitter, holy bitter, holy bitter.'

I pad down the stairs to the kitchen and open my notebook. There they are, the words as I last wrote them. And now I knew what they were…abortifacients. At the sound of the word, a ripple moves across my stomach like my baby is reading my thoughts, reading my notebook, urging me to shut it and go back to bed, sleep like a proper wife beside my husband until a decent hour wakes us to a godly day.

'Hush, hush,' I murmur, stroking my belly. I pick up the pen and write, 'Searching for Judith,' in big bold letters.

'Abortifacients,' I write. 'Is this the key, Judith? What are you trying to tell me?'

'Do you dare summon me, a madwoman, to your kitchen table?'

'I want your story, Judith. I want to know why you came to me in that symphony. What is it you are meant to be? I…I demand to know.'

'All right, if you "demand" it.' Again that tone, laden with mockery. *'Eve, I am a woman derailed. I was set on the*

track much like you were. I was polished. I was painted a bonny bright-red engine and sent puffing along to tie bows on bunches of flowers; to hold my spine in a plumbline posture; cream-clean my face, gently patting the eyelids with alternating fingerprint pads, cooling, tightening, stimulating lotions closing my pores; not a sissy about outdoor sports; vivacity, charm; brushing shiny teeth, sides of bristles against the gum tissue at a forty-five-degree angle, tufts pointing towards biting edge of teeth; holding in waist; snipping my split ends. Did you know a normal scalp can lose up to fifty hairs a day, and keep them replaced? Autumn and spring there's an even higher turnover, so don't be alarmed at a good crop in that hairbrush; two lemons to two glasses of water for shine but quickly rinse out so I don't smell like a salad! I'm developing personality in my hair! Am I a better-looking girl now? I study my face for my special assets. What shall I make up, what shall I make down. Never slipshod. I won't be any man's favourite White Collar Girl if my collar shows yesterday's grime. Brush out my hair, into my date dress, now comb hair into shape — one last blot of lipstick…Ready: lights, camera! Bzz-zz-zz. There's his ring. He's here!'

'Who's here, Judith?'

'Why, my man of course, ready to take me out to my first party. Do you know how to make a man feel comfortable at a party? Does he seem tired, rather nervous and drawn-looking? Put him with the least possible fuss into a chair, open a box of cigarettes beside him and ask, "Highball or martini?" and then get it as quickly as possible. If he seems bright and bustling, say, "I'm so glad you're here. Would you mind making me a martini? Mine are not as good as yours." This makes him feel important. To put a woman at ease, simply say something flattering, admire her hat. That's the same as a stiff drink for a man — a spirit-lifter! You look fine today, Eve. I

know it's cold, but the bracing air only makes you look better! Or would you prefer a stiff drink?'

'So you went to parties and married the man?'

'You catch on quickly, Eve. Do you know the married working woman is largely responsible for many of our national ills: disturbed personalities, broken homes, divorce, juvenile delinquency? I read that once: disturbed personalities, delinquency...It's true, too. I should know.'

'Did you feel disturbed?'

'My, my, only a pretty face. No, Eve, darling, I burnt the house down for kicks. I didn't work. My husband wouldn't allow it. He was a doctor, you know, just like yours. It's dangerous to leave a woman alone too long, don't you think, Eve? We're such chaotic creatures!

'I became bored. Terribly bored and you remember the grime, don't you? And my doctor, he made love like a doctor. You know what I mean, don't you, Eve? Coldly, from seeing so many bodies. From having them dissected for him, anatomised. And you are a diagram lying flat on your back. Your form, your curves, are anomalies he studies. He professes passion but in his eyes there's only bewilderment, despite all his medical texts. He's not quite sure what to do with you. Professor, can we have a demonstration? A model. And you lie there like a cadaver. You can't tell me he satisfies.'

'You are cruel, too cruel.' My pen is possessed. Never before have I written such things, blasphemous, pitiless things!

'So I had affairs, Eve. Many of them. With many men. And my doctor, he called me a whore, an evil witch, an ungodly woman, mad! But what can I say, Eve? You should never leave a woman to her own devices in a life as miniature as that! A toy doll in a toy house.'

'But the baby? There was a baby, yes?'

The pen freezes in my hand. Judith walks out of the kitchen down to the lake. She lies down on the grass, black hair falling like a curtain across her face. Our conversation, it is clear, is over.

Despite the heat from the oven, my breath hangs in a frosted cloud from my lips. There is no movement or sound. I stare at the empty space at the bottom of my page and the question left lingering…a sigh…an accusation? I feel my baby move again. I look down and see its foot, or is it a hand, slide across the inside of my stomach. Who is this small stranger inside me, so obstinate, so firm? Does it think me a bad mother? I shut the notebook. As I switch the kettle on, I hear the padding of Todd's feet down the hall. His face peers in, puffy with sleep.

'Bad dream, Mummy,' he says, flinging himself into my arms. I hold him for a while as he grips me so tight I can see his knuckles whiten.

'There, there, only a dream. Everything's all right now.' I rub his back, feeling his shoulder blades, bony and shivering beneath his pyjamas. 'Do you want to tell Mummy?'

He shakes his head.

'Look, do you want to feel the baby kick? It's very lively this morning.'

Todd's face lights up instantly. Whatever terrible dream he had floods from his memory with this new distraction. He places his hand on my stomach.

'Don't feel nothin',' He whispers.

'Wait a moment.'

He bends towards me, listening, brow creased with the effort. 'There it goes, I felt it!' He giggles and starts running around the kitchen. 'It's a baby! It's a baby!'

'Quietly, your father's sleeping.' I pour milk into a glass for him.

He stops running. 'Does it have any toys in there?' he asks, eyes wide with the sad thought of no toys for the baby.

'I'm sure it has plenty of toys.'

I wish it were as easy for me to forget bad dreams as it is for Todd.

I spend that afternoon out in the garden. I weed between the tomatoes and carrot stalks. It is good to get down in the earth pulling the roots, clearing the ground. After the icy morning, the sun has come out to play. It is a strange country; so contradictory. Right in the middle of summer one could still wake up to dew frozen into icicle spears. All the cherry blossoms have lost their petals now and stretch bare-limbed, stripped of their ball gowns. The wisteria is still blooming alongside the sweet peas and marigolds. It is a reprieve to be here, hidden among the fruit trees and spinach.

After clearing the patch, I sit beneath my favourite tree, a pink melaleuca. Just to the side of it springs a white star-flowered eriostemon. It is the most private spot in the garden, hedged in by bushes and plum trees. None of the neighbours can see in here, not Toby nor Mrs Brent. Richard wanted to cut my melaleuca down, something about the roots growing under the house. I got upset about it though and he said, 'We'll see, we'll see...' in the tone he uses with his patients.

Sometimes I tried to write here but my head would fly off with the bees, or a bird nesting in the branches. Even a wind tossing the leaves of the melaleuca could carry away my thoughts. Today, though, I keep coming back to Judith and the strange things she is saying, the strange things I am writing with this bitter tongue, this wicked tongue. I am happy. I have Richard, my home, Todd, a new baby. I couldn't be happier, surely?

Richard says he worries at times about my nerves. After Todd was born, he even gave me some pills to help me sleep, but I was just sensitive. That's what he said, sensitive as all women are. Delicate…I remember how he stroked my cheek as he said that…delicate.

At times I've laughed a little too loudly in company, found it just bursting out of me, and Richard reaches across and pats my hand. He always watches how many martinis I have at parties and tells me, 'That's enough, darling,' at times taking away my drink if he decides he needs to.

And then that night at the Randalls', I got so caught up in the music I didn't even help Valerie whip the cream! Richard always says writing is too introverted to be a healthy sport.

'Aren't all writers mad?'

I decide not to think. I am thinking too much. I will make jam instead; that will settle my nerves. I pick some rhubarb and go inside. I uncover the bowl of loganberries I stewed the night before and pull open the recipe drawer, finding the one from the Pialba State School Ladies' Auxiliary a girlfriend of mine sent me. I check the measurements. I notice my girlfriend has underlined a paragraph above the steps for jellied pineapple and under the recipe for rhubarb and loganberry jam.

How to preserve a husband

Be careful of your selection. Take only those that have been grown in a good moral atmosphere. Do not use too young, slightly matured. When selected, do not keep them in a pickle or hot water; this tends to make them sour, hard and sometimes bitter. Most varieties can be made sweet and tender by garnishing with patience, well sweetened with smiles and flavoured to taste with kisses. Then wrap in a mantle of charity, keep warm with a steady fire of devotion, and serve with peaches and cream. When thus served they will keep for years.

Sweet and tender, charitable, devoted? I do try to be. I try not to complain or nag or be difficult. A good moral atmosphere? I thought so, but Judith?

'*Would you like to preserve a husband?*' I hear her voice over my shoulder. '*I like to pickle them myself, or stew them. That way they have more bite when you dish them up!*'

I cannot help but laugh. Judith says things I would not dare say. I imagine her waving a red flag, addressing strangers in the street, walking about with her nails ragged, her clothes untidy, sleeping at odd times of the day, allowing strange men to…I concentrate on the recipe – wash and cut rhubarb into inch lengths. Boil with one pound sugar and one tablespoon lemon juice. Slowly stir and dissolve sugar. Add loganberries when rhubarb is soft. Bring to boil again.

As the sugar dissolves, the smell of soft boiling fruit fills the kitchen. I stand over the pot stirring and stirring, eyes watching the swirling black liquid as it turns thicker and thicker. It grows hot in the kitchen, the air pungent and oppressive. It has a decadent smell, jam, rich and full…so sweet, almost sickly. It reminds me of the honey milk that came from my breast when I was feeding Todd…sticky, clinging to the skin. I can smell it now, I am sure of it. The smell of milk and the sound of crying, a moaning cry of something newborn…Judith's baby? I stop stirring and grab my pen. I start writing, a stream of words flying fast.

'*The baby was not meant to be. I could feel it. An alien thing growing in my body. I had lost the final frontier, my final boundary to the conquering world that ripped everything else out of me. Now they put something inside me. What should I do? What should I do? Doctor wants it, says he'll keep it, doesn't matter who the real father is. What's he doing with a wife like me? Why does he keep giving? Doesn't he know I'm bad? He gives me pills, so many pills, but they can't keep my head at bay. And now they've planted something inside me. I'm going to have to care for it every hour, every day. I'm not fit to look after myself let alone another thing like that, clingy, defenceless. It's happened before, the sickness in the morning, the stopping of the blood. I took herbs, holy bitter, an apt name for such foul poison. But he found out. He took it away. Had me watched like an animal, said I wasn't going to get this one.*

'*A murderess? He's called me that before, when he first found out. All the babies he didn't know about slipping quietly into darkness, holy bitter, holy bitter. But if my belly was too far gone, then came the butchers with metal teeth, raring to grab it out of you for a price. Jam it up you. Leave you bloody, knotted. He's going to save this one, he said, make us whole, like a family, round and good and whole. I'll be a proper mother, he said, or else…What? Is he losing his patience? Is he going to lock me up? Doesn't he love me any more? He never believed me about the fire. Everyone else did but he never did. An accident? He asked but it was the way he asked like he knew, and he never said any more. Then the baby! Got to get it out of me. Is he losing love for me, my doctor?*

'*He's the only one and then…what comes for me? All the men I've had don't care. They don't look me in the eye. Their honeysuckle wives grab their arms and they hurry past me in the*

street like I'm poison and we don't get invited to parties any more,
no martinis for me, "but you make them so much better than I do,
here would you like a seat, a cigarette?" and doctor says he's losing
work but he says we could move, maybe I need fresh air, he says,
live by a lake, he says, and trees. That'll get you right...it's just
your nerves, darling, that's what he'll say, just your nerves, you're
so sensitive, delicate, he kisses me light as fairy floss, sweet sweet so
sticky and my stomach's swelling, pumped out. I don't look like me.
I am a strange girl. I got the pain. I didn't tell. Got past the nurse
he sent to watch me. She thinks I'm a nice girl. She doesn't know
me, fooled her, fooled her! Got down by the lake. Hid in the bushes
and out it came. The pain! The bastard. But I didn't let them get
it, no I didn't let them get me, no I put it in the lake and it didn't
even cry, well maybe just a bit, just a little bit. Do you hear it? Do
you hear it, Eve? Smells like your jam is burning.'

That night I stay up after Richard and Todd go to bed. I
sit in the kitchen, moving the lamp in from the lounge so I
can see better at night. I see her at eight riding her bicycle,
pigtails flying, laughing at a big man with one arm. Her
father, she says, a war hero, lots of medals, all gold like
money on his chest, and she would stroke them and want her
own medals. She would marry a man with lots of gold like
that and a broad chest to squeeze. Daddy, Daddy, Daddy...As
late spring turns to summer, we fill notebook after notebook,
her life swelling with my own pregnant belly. We would be
up many nights past midnight, then slipping into bed, quiet
as a mouse. She wanted to go on but I had to push her away,
pushed her.

My eyes opening to the dim light, creeping down into
the kitchen, my fingers sore, knuckles bent, we would chase
the thread where we left it, a whole ball of yarn coming

undone, picking at the knots, scraping her story together in patches. She is patchy, Judith, but she hangs herself together. Times, though, she would not come and I sat there alone weaving the thread until I drew her to me. She chased herself away, scared of what was coming next – a hurt, a death, deceit. I never thought she could be scared, my bold Judith, but she is.

I struggled with her too. Why could she not be happy contained in a good life? A good marriage? It is natural to be a mother. Why resist? Warping to badness, madness? I wanted to plead, offer some excuse for her reckless indifference to all that was proper. Maybe it is in the genes, the blood. Tainted stock from birth, as the scientists say? Less choice than the rest of us?

'*Pump it out, Eve, that's right, pump us clean! Pat pat pitter patter, can you hear the lady say? Pat in even circular motion along the cheekbones, girls. Pump those pores clean! A lifetime's accumulation of oil, dirt, dead cells! That's what I am, Eve, a lifetime's accumulation!*'

She would laugh then and smile, that one that barely turned her lips up. '*Maybe,*' she would say, nodding her head. '*I should have been sedated and locked up long ago.*' But she looked at me like I had missed something, the final one to not live up to her grand expectations of life, the glitter of medals, the heroes, the gold. I had to watch she did not grow too large. I felt at times she could consume me. She would joke, saying she could eat me up. All her words were double-edged.

Sometimes Todd woke early and I would draw funny faces in the margins to keep him quiet. One morning, he was playing with a tin tray, filling it with stones, scraping it up and down, to make what he thought was a beautiful noise. No chance of us working, so I sketched his face as he sat there on the kitchen floor. It looked otherworldly in the dawn light. Angelic, the small chin, smooth the skin... Other times, when we were chasing the threads, we were less patient. The sound of Todd's feet coming down the hall was a death knell and I would have to stop Judith swiping him down as one would a fly.

I existed only in those blue hours. Outside of them, I was so tired. Richard chided me constantly, exhorting me to look after my unborn child if not myself. He claimed the housework was suffering too. At the Randalls', I drank too many martinis. I would not let Richard take them away. And I laughed so loudly that I saw them looking at me the way Judith must have felt so many times. Richard told them it was my nerves with the pregnancy. I knew it was Judith.

One time we even took the phone off the hook and told Richard I had been on the phone to the grocer. I could not stop writing. I walked with Judith through all the back alleys of her life. Her lifetime accumulation of dead cells, as she would say. I watched her destroy those who loved her. I watched her cast aside the goodness of life to taste bitterness. Richard gave me pills I pretended to swallow. Judith spat them out the minute he was gone.

It was autumn by the time I finished. I stretched out the ending for a good while. I knew she would have to die. I would have to kill her. There was nowhere else for her to go. What happens to a woman who cannot be a good wife, a good mother? What else is there? And yet so much pain as I saw her lying there on the linoleum floor. The gas from the oven filled the kitchen till not a breath was left.

The doors were sealed so there was no leakage of air. Even now she would not lie properly. She must sprawl out on the floor, abandoned, triumphant, ruined for all to see. Her robe falling off her shoulder, indecent to the end. Always the last words were hers. And the look she gave me…She knew what I had done. I had no medals for her. I had no heroics. I had given her up too easily, she would say, just like all the rest. But she was beyond redemption…It was mercy…it was merciful.

I had not wanted to leave her. Not like this. I sit for such a time, the pen suspended above the paper, searching for another resolution, another point of ending. There is no way to elude her fate. Yet her ghost has not been laid to rest. Judith would never be a restful spirit. I can still call her up with those opening chords of Tchaikovsky's 6th Symphony. She loves the magnificence of the classics, the outrageous tragedy. She made me vow to learn the piano and I think I shall. She says we will play like madwomen, all of Tchaikovsky and perhaps even a little Bach.

Outside the glass, autumn leaves spill in fountains from the trees like gold rain – an airborne funeral procession. And there is Todd walking up the path. Home from school, satchel smacking against his leg. So frail, his body against the trunks and branches. Relentless too, those thick short legs coming home for tea, coming home to me.

Between the Chapters...

Sybylla has collapsed in the garden bed. She lies sprawled out in the marigolds; dark smears of what looks like mascara stain her eyes. Her fingers are curled in the dirt and her skirt has fallen up over her knees. I bend down close and put my hand to her lips. There is no warm air coming from her mouth. I smell gas in her clothes, in her hair. The same smell that filled Judith's kitchen.

'We have to get out of this together. I need you.' I whisper in her ear.

Slowly the blood starts returning to her cheeks. She shivers and I hold her up to me, against me. As the colour comes back to her face, the darkness around her eyes fades. She begins to look like herself again, the slope of her forehead, the shape of her cheekbones.

'I'm still here?' She pats the dirt around her.

'Yes, you're all right.'

'I should never have stayed to the end of that story. Not in this time. They always kill the woman in the end. I was just hoping…' Sybylla pauses and her eyes grow wider. 'I thought maybe she wouldn't kill me this time…and I warned you about getting too close.'

'Don't talk. Just rest a moment.'

I want to move her away from this flowerbed, away from this garden and this house. We are too exposed out here, like bugs that can be seen by any bird. I look up. There is a bird now in the sky. It stretches its wings. I'm sure it is circling over the house. Sybylla looks so small I can pick her up. I gather her in my arms and stumble out of the front yard with her. She is almost weightless. It is strange to walk down a street in suburbia like this. All the rows of brick-veneer houses with the same curtains, same patios, even the same hedges in their front yards. What would the neighbours think of such a sight? A woman carrying another woman, both of them looking a little crazed and the worse for wear.

One of the neighbours pulls into the driveway opposite in a big green Ford. He doesn't appear to see us. We pass a woman with a pram and an elderly man. No one looks in our direction. We are invisible. The only time I think we are seen is when a curtain moves in the front window of one of the houses. There is a young girl standing behind it. I see her smile at us and then hide again behind the curtain veil.

Finally, as I am about to rest on the footpath, we come upon a park. There are barbecues, a swing and a shelter for the rain. I lay Sybylla on a bench under the shelter. She rests her head on my lap. I sit there stroking her hair. I watch as a family walks into the park. They are having a barbecue for dinner. There is a dog and two children are racing around the swings. The mum is unpacking all the Tupperware and the dad is greasing the barbecue. My memories of childhood are not that far from these. The smell of the sausages sizzling makes me long for the time I was running around parks, safe as these two children. I don't know if they have seen us. One of them, the youngest, a chubby girl with pigtails in pink velvet bows, has looked our way. She is trying to throw a ball that is almost as big as her.

The mum is buttering bread rolls now. She is laughing as the girl almost falls over the ball as she tries to pick it up. The other child, her older brother, kicks it away from her just when she is about to get a firm hold on it. I think he has spotted us too. He keeps looking this way with a curious grin.

Sybylla stirs. She raises a hand to her mouth. 'Mmm, that barbecue smells good.'

'No, no more dinners for you in this time. You've had quite enough,' I say.

She sits up and eyes the woman at the picnic table. 'All right,' she says, 'I'll be good.'

I want to ask what happened, why her face changed and how she became a stranger. How did she creep into Eve's mind? Is Sybylla the muse? Or the instigator, the creator? But I do not have a chance. Our movement on the bench has caught the little girl's attention. She waddles over, shuffling her ball in front of her. She stands and watches us for some time, her fingers stuck in her mouth. Her eyes take in everything: our shoes, our hair, the shiny ring on my finger. She is like a magpie. She doesn't miss a thread. She seems particularly fascinated by Sybylla and keeps staring at her. I can see the mum looking over. Then the child smiles and her dimples spring out, lighting up her face.

'You wanna come play on shwing?' She points over to the swing set, her pudgy fingers covered in saliva.

Sybylla gives her a big smile back. 'Sure.'

'Are you sure you should be walking around…' I know I am fussing but I can't help it.

'I'll be fine.' She gives me a wink.

I watch as the child wriggles onto the seat of the swing. Sybylla is behind her. She starts pushing the girl gradually at first, a little swing. Then I see her bending down, whispering in the child's ear. The little girl starts to laugh. The swing starts to fly higher and higher. The boy has gone to help his dad with the meat, and the mum is setting the picnic table with knives and forks. I can see the mum's face. She is looking over at the swings. Her brow is creased and I can see she is staring. It does not surprise her that the girl appears to be chatting to no one in particular. That is what children do. What she cannot work out is how the swing is getting higher when the girls legs are too short to push it that close to the sky. On top of which the girl is not even pushing her legs back and forth. She has them stuck out in front of her and the swing is not even riding backward to the same extent that it moves forwards.

'Susie, Susie,' the mum calls. 'It's almost time for dinner. Susie come and let me wipe your hands.'

There is something about this time of the evening, dusk, that makes her nervous. It is not a time when children are meant to be swinging so high. It is a time when, for all the vegemite and cheese sandwiches in the world, one does not feel quite safe. The girl ignores her and the swing keeps flying higher. Even I am starting to worry that the little girl might slip off, that some terrible accident might happen.

She looks tiny on the seat as she lurches forward in the air. Sybylla claps her hands. She is laughing as she pushes the child. I walk over to them to warn her about the mother.

I can hear the girl calling, '*Birdie, Birdie.*'

And Sybylla is singing something. It sounds like a folk song or a nursery rhyme. '*Fly high, Birdie, fly high. To the sky. To the sky. Birdie, Birdie gonna fly high. Gonna fly high, to the sky.*'

As my eyes follow the swinging child to the sky, I see the bird again, the one that was circling us when we were on the hill, in the garden bed. I can't believe it has followed us. It is circling around and around.

'Quickly,' Sybylla says to me, 'Get on the other swing. I'll push you!'

I start to say this is nonsense and the mum is worried, she had better let the child down and stop swinging her so high. But for some reason I don't. The most I can utter is 'But...' I sit down on the seat of the other swing and in between pushing the child, Sybylla begins to push me. It feels so bizarre to be a grown woman on a swing.

I am moving faster and faster now, my hands around the metal links. I can hear the creak in the hinges that strap the swings into the frame. As I come forward, the girl goes backwards. She is squealing in delight, eyes sparkling like glass marbles. She looks over to me as if we share a secret joke. I find myself laughing too. When I let myself relax, I remember how good it feels to play like this. It does feel like flying. Sybylla is still singing her 'Birdie, Birdie' song, and I do feel like a bird. I catch sight of the bird above me and stop fearing it. We are not so far apart. We could be kin. I could be up there flying with spread-eagled wings.

The girl and I start moving in unison, so now we come forward together and swing back at the same time. I see the mum running over. She looks like a dot on the grass. I don't believe she matters at all. We are so high. We are free of everyone and everything. I turn around to laugh again with the girl. But the girl has vanished. Instead, Sybylla perches in the swing. She grins at me.

'Take my hand,' she says. On the count of three, jump!' I take her hand.

'One, two,' she waits until we are at the highest point in the air, 'three!'

We let go of the metal chains holding the swing. We are flying through the sky. Everything moves so fast. Clouds skate past. Then I see the shape of a house, the red-tiled roof as we come nearer, then a window frame, an open window to an attic. We hurtle through it and land with a thud on a wooden floor. There is a young woman sitting in front of a fireplace. The fireplace is empty. It looks like it has not burnt wood for years.

Instead she crouches beside an electric heater. In front of her is an old red hatbox. It looks as though it has weathered many hats, though there is no hat in it now, only paper spilling out of it onto the floor. It is clear from the way the pages are strewn about that the woman has been reading them. She does not look alarmed by our curious entrance.

I am now used to meeting women unexpectedly, but there is something familiar about this one. I only realise what it is when she looks up and smiles. Her eyes are shiny and she still has the dimples and curly hair of the girl on the swing. She must be about thirty years older now. Not much younger than me. The smile is the same but there is a difference. Although her eyes are still bright, there are walls in them. It is hard to see right through. The brightness, too, has changed. It is less like glass catching the sun and more like lava or something volcanic. It has a bitter edge, a little too bright, too combustible.

'Susie, look at you all grown up!' Sybylla goes towards her, bends down and gives her a hug. Susie puts her arms around Sybylla and holds her tight. They stay like that for a moment. Then Sybylla turns and motions for me to sit down next to them on the rug.

'Ah, Birdie lady,' Susie says. 'I've been waiting for you. You gotta light?'

Sybylla pulls out her box of matches.

'Thanks.'

Susie places a cigarette between her lips and lights it with the match. She keeps the match burning, watching as the flame creeps closer to her skin. With her other hand she picks out a scrap of paper from the hatbox as though she were drawing a lottery. Her story is pieced together from poems and thoughts she has stored in this box. As she unfolds each piece of paper, she lays it like part of a map in front of her on the floor. It is as if she is using her words to find her way back from somewhere strange and far away. She says she is piecing her life back together.

'My body of work.' She looks up with a grin. 'It's good to have company.' She blows out the match just as the flame reaches her fingers.

Susanne 1979

What's a good Catholic girl to do with her undies wet at five? Peeing whenever the good doctor comes around to examine me. Now I would say piss. I'm not a good Catholic girl now. I piss. I don't pee. I piss like a man. I don't procreate. I fuck. I do not have secret bits with rabbit names like 'munni'. I have a cunt. Did you know Cunti was a goddess? I would be arrested for swearing now if a cop happened to brush by me on the street as I was letting off steam. I would be offending the public. I would be locked up. So easy to be filthy when invoking a goddess is 'foul language'. See, that's where that thought started. My cunt leads me to my first memory.

A man fat as an overstuffed teddy bear lurches out of the pub. Spews all over my new buckle shoes and my bobby socks with their trimming of lace. He doesn't pause to mutter an apology. I step on by, Mum leading me quickly by the hand. This was swill time when the pubs closed at six. They ripped out all the insides to make space for the hordes gulping down their numbing slop in the barns. Then they hose it out. A trough for the beasts that are our men, coming home, toppling, to take their place at the head of the table.

My dad comes home swaying. He's about to topple sideways. Hey ho and up she rises. Down he goes to the dunny. He doesn't make it in time. Fortunately, my bobby socks are out of the way. Mum turns, pretends he's sick a lot. 'Sorry kids, sorry kids.' She irons us all out. Spends all her time pressing and heaving and sighing. Her smile is stuck to her face like candy. She draws it on in rose-red lippy. You know when Cyclone Tracy tore through Darwin, the government sent the women boxes of lippy. For their self-esteem, you know. Bugger that. If anyone gave me lippy after I'd been tossed in a cyclone, I'd fucken sock 'em.

Maybe that's the way I am, though. I need more than a stick of red paste to cheer me up, make me pretty. And what'd these women say? Hey, I've lost my house, got no food, got no nappies for the baby, it's shitting all over the place but at least I look good for my man. He'll still want to screw me. Talk about band-aid and a stiff upper lip. But it's not all bad. They've promised to stop naming cyclones after women. The next one's going to be a man. It'll be cyclone Jeff lifting up your roof. Some consolation when you're sitting in your chimney, with your stick of lippy. That's what we get for the Year of the Bird, though. A whole 365 days dedicated to women to make up for the thousands of years taken by men. That should right things up, hey. Keep you girls happy. Stop ya nagging. Shut ya up.

I reckon women's lib can be seen in the stages of bicycles, slacks, smokes and sex. The last is still in question but we've certainly got the smoking down pat. Tobacco companies have made a mint out of women's lib as we rebel women inhale freedom from all that nicotine. My sisters and I are smoking chimneys, revelling in our dad's disapproving face, our mothers 'tut'. Our revolution is being built to the staccato coughing of black tar from liberated lungs. We still do what good girls don't and in a way it's sad to get your strength from that. Reactionary, that'd be the word for it. I feel like a constant bloody reaction. Corsets are still worn, just not seen. I feel the strings pull at my lungs every time I breathe in this stinking place where Darwin's theory of evolution is well and truly rooted.

My story does not begin one fine spring day in May. I cannot pin my stories down. They prick me if I thread them anyway that makes sense. So I am senseless, knocked out for the count. I like it that way. It's true to the tale. This old hatbox was Mum's. I took it when she died. It was the only thing in the house that reminded me of her. She did not wear hats as far as I can remember. This one was empty. The only clue is a photo of her, a young trim thing, a pretty floral bit of straw and lace on her head. Eyes alight for the camera. Smiling secretly, alive before I knew her. If I ever really did.

The box is filled now, with my papers. Scraps of thoughts penned in hard times, when I boiled up enough to squirt something on the page. I string them together now. I'm not sure what I'm looking for. I don't have photos 'cept that one of Mum. Never bothered with a camera. Thought it would spoil the moment to capture it and try to hold it down.

Instead I have poems, plays…scribbled drivel, rants, raves. I started loving words about the time I met you at the park. I could barely talk right, but I caught onto sounds and songs like that rhyme you were singing – '*Birdie, Birdie, fly high… gonna fly Birdie to the sky…*' I found poetry that day. On that swing with you. Flying so high I was a bird. After that I had more magic times. I remember I was playing with marbles, frozen worlds inside glass. They sent me flying...

> *The magic is in the glass. Holding to my ear the eggshells from the kitchen roar with sea and sand lifts the vinyl from the floor, the linoleum I thought would drown me is instead overcome by marbles, shells and glassy creatures that say I could slide small as a sliver between the holes of the cheese grater, scramble over the table and high foot it to the clothes line where swinging, feet free of the grass, I sail past the pegs and way off into the blue.*

'Susie, Susie!' Mum's screech barely grazes my wings.

When I could read, I read a book about a horse. I cried. Couldn't believe books, those flat dead things, could make you cry. I decided I was going to be the heroine of my story:

> *She holds her pen like a sword. She's a swashbuckling hero. She's a pirate stealing from the rich to give to the poor. She cuts sugarcane like candy. Forests fall to the floor. Her blade has wings. Sometimes you can see her at night, riding her silver sickle to the moon. Dare say she could slice armies, most probably does. She goes into battle. Pride pinned to her chest. Thrusting, jabbing but more often slashing, she cuts through fabrics of worlds, lies, oceans of glass illusion. Her teeth shatter stone.*

But there weren't any heroines I wanted to be. I didn't want to faint or get kidnapped. There were only heroes. Like my brother who doesn't have to do the dishes. Once I started writing I could not stop. The more life hemmed me in the more I wrote till it was chasing me. I was stuck with it.

There it was again: the hissing beneath the sheets, the itching steam rising from my head every time I looked at the yellow grass backyards and the women with trolleys and prams, shopping bags banging on thighs. Women with minds as pressed and dried as the flowers they used books to weigh down. This place grew smaller every time I blinked and I grew so large with all the gas of bottled dreams I thought I would blow myself and the flower women to shreds.

Being a girl stinks. Freud's right. I want a penis. It's your free ticket anywhere.

Ink stains
spurt on her blue velvet breast

She's been playing
with her penis again
thrilling to its rapid strokes
on pale virgin paper

There a mark
a birth
a word
stolen from this tool of men
heaven help her
she'll never be sated by silence again!

By the time I left school, I needed a ticket out desperately. Dad and I had become war veterans in opposite camps. Every time I went out he would start on me. Something nice like 'little slut' under his breath. When he was more grogged up,

he would extend his vocabulary: 'Bitch…whore…tramp…
tart. Look at what she's wearing…You're not half what your
mum is!'

I'd slam the door.

Mum would chase after me. 'He doesn't know what he's
saying. It's a sickness.'

Right, Mum. Funny how everything he could swing at
me had to do with sex. I was still a virgin, kind of…if you
don't count the stuff when I was a kid. I should've died. If I
was a good girl, I would have fought and died like St Maria,
that peasant girl in Italy. We were given a leaflet about her at
school, with her mum saying how proud she was her child
got murdered rather than got herself raped and have to live
to tell the tale – death before honour. The church canonised
her. Twelve years old and such virtue. My life was nothing
to anyone, not like my 'chastity', and I had lost that already.
On the rocks down at the beach. Wasn't my fault but I was
dirty. She was pure. She was a saint. What was I? What a
load of crap, hey? But you don't know that then. So when
Dad called me names, a bit did stick…sticks 'n stones may
break my bones…but names…

I applied to Sydney University. It was far away from here
and they offered me a teaching scholarship, a good job for a
girl. My first week there, I saw the Miss Fresher contest. The
prettiest first-year girls competed for the title. They walked
down the length of a catwalk in the gymnasium to a chorus
of wolf whistles. A girl I'd just met, Betty, entered herself
into it. She was thrilled. I said it was cheap. She told me I
was jealous and ugly. It was a short friendship.

Between cramming, I went on dates with 'nice' boys. I
got a chance to do all that fighting I hadn't done when I was

a kid. We'd go out for dinner, maybe a movie. They'd pull over and park on the way home. All that civilised crap got tossed out the window and you spent twenty minutes while they forced themselves on you and you tried to hold onto your 'reputation'. And then I lost the fight…

> *This doom man*
> *Pumping ferociously*
> *above my head*

Fucken' pigs. What I'd do to 'em now if I had the chance. Back then I was still a 'nice girl'. I thought long and hard about this second loss of virginity. I thought about St Maria. I thought about whether it was worth dying for. Not likely!

I got the idea the only way to get heard on campus or off was to *use* your sex. I started to dress differently. Put on more make-up, wear tighter tops. I went to a pub where the women were supposed to get treated like the men and there was loads of great talk: politics, philosophy, the lot. They called themselves the 'Push'. Only 'bad' girls were meant to hang out there, but I was fast losing my 'good girl' status. I went with Mandy, a friend who was dating one of the Push crew. Mandy and I were not valued for our intellectual assets, however, and while the talk was great it was often one-sided. I would find myself frequently on the butt end of a diatribe:

> *You're lulling me to sleep with your politics, your talk and your self-infatuation. I wouldn't interrupt for the world. Where does it all come from, this wheezing, when you barely notice the person you're talking to? Habitual padding from a well of women has*

*been your downfall. Women to milk, dress, feed and ply you all
the way through school and into the big wide cradle, made specially
for bores like you. I lean a little cleavage into the conversation, and
find there is at least one thing that pierces the self-absorption of the
man across from me. Maybe this is the key to getting a word in.*

The other girls seemed happy to hang on every word as it
dripped from their men's mouths. They were happy even to
be allowed in. They thought all the 'free sex' was free, and if
they felt bartered around and never had an orgasm 'cause the
fucks were so quick, they thought *they* were 'dysfunctional'.
But it wasn't so fine with me. It had to do with some women
I'd noticed on campus.

I saw them first at the Miss Fresher contest in second year.
They sat on the catwalk and held the whole show up. The
boys got really pissed off, yelling 'n throwing things at them.
But the women kept on chanting 'Stop exploiting women'
and 'We are not objects for your pleasure'. They were
handing out leaflets. The boys tore them up. I kept mine.

I went to one of their meetings. It was different. They sat
around on the floor in a circle. There was no leader. They
just talked and listened. You'd think it would be chaos but
it was pretty calm. I mean, we were excited, really excited
at times, but no one was jostling for space. No one wanted
all the attention. It wasn't a competition. You didn't have
to scream or manoeuvre yourself into conversation. It just
went around and all the women got a turn. They let you
speak and there was just this knowing that you were sharing
space and time and not to get greedy when you were talking.
And it wasn't like school – there was no hands-up sort of
thing – or too polite. They weren't polite at all...There was

'shit that', and 'fuck that' and a lot about 'bloody males'. It was the first time I saw and felt respect. Real respect, not the stuff they beat out of you, to give to them and none of it kept for yourself:

> *...Can you feel the beating bushes in your head straining thought past the reach of its branches, a new leaf pushes against air into birth,*

> > *the bushes bend under the weight of another strange notion of who and what you are.*

Stuff made sense.

The screws came loose

> *My girdle burst*

Boobs popped open

> *Vagina cracked*

Tin and aluminium casing

> > *Smacked the floor*

My knees blew

          Moments before collapse

I stopped reading the great men: Hemingway, Lawrence, Byron, Henry James, Joyce. I started digesting *The Second Sex*. I stopped wearing make-up. Women became sisters. Joan, Casey, Anne, Marg – all my sisters now. We were trying to find words for what we wanted. We were working to define that word, 'Liberation'…from what, for what?

> *…I gave voice to it honey and it sung like a dove but it weren't*
> *flying for peace, no, it was out for blood!*
> *Do we leave bloodstains on the carpet*
> *thoughtlessly dripping over the fine pile*
> *with our runny pens*
> *calling attention to ourselves?*
> *Do we get in the way?*
> *Our bodies taking space up in the boot?*
> *Easily done but not so easily disposable.*
> *Our drip drip*
> *calls attention to ink splodges*
> *where words should be,*
> *a name where there is a nobody.*
> *Did we disrupt the party?*
> *Stop behaving like the good escorts*
> *we are supposed to be?*
> *Did we drink too much*

and take ourselves out alone?
Did we ravage the streets
until all innocents were slain?
Did we make a mess?
Did we ignore you?
Make you feel smaller
than you're used to?
Whatever it is,
it must be a heinous crime
To make you work
at being bastards overtime.

I was pissed off. And I got more pissed off the more us women came together. The stories we told would fold and lap over each other, weaving this picture that had been standing right before our eyes but we couldn't see it 'cause we were pitted against each other like cocks in a ring, tearing at each other over keepin' our man. But we weren't cocks, right? I mean we didn't have a cock. That was the point. I started thinking about the way I felt in this man's world. Always unsafe. Always watching my back on enemy ground…ever since that day on the beach…

and the ground never changes 'cause the whole world is round, so
baby I'm just gonna go round in circles. No matter where I stand
I'm on man's land. There is no no man's land. That's a juicy
trick to get us running…

I scull
my drink
the way a deer

gulps down
the afterbirth

No bear or
lion is going
to catch
the stink
of my soft dumbness

Or are those eyes there
checking out the scene
and my coat
wandering over my form?
And then
I am a fawn
bolting from the bar
scared from my safe
squatting in the long grass

Now alone in the dark
my long legs strike against gravel
snake rattle of keys on fingers
and behind
behind
is there a beast?
The click of the carnivore?
Or my own praying mantis
my stalky shadow
scaring itself stupid?

I tried to get my poems into women's mags – *Me Jane*, *Refractory Girl* and the like. I read them out loud at women's nights. A lot of us wrote. Some of my sisters started writing for the first time in their lives. They had been too scared before. Didn't even think it was something they could do. The stuff about the personal being political was a chant to us; it kept us from letting in the world as we had known it, the world that told us what we were saying was crap and didn't mean shit. The world as men liked it to be. I read out poems about how hard I was finding it to practise my newfound theories. For all the reinvention I was feeling inside, I still acted like a 'lady' on the outside.

It hit me when a man walked straight into me in the Manning caf. He didn't even glance down, just kept going, his elbows knocking coffee over my shirt. And I said sorry! Like it was my fault! Like I was in the way of his natural right to walk anywhere. And he just kept on walking! I was left with my stained shirt and half-empty cup of coffee.

She thought her existence was the greatest breach of etiquette in history. 'I really must apologise for my lateness.' She was on time. 'I really must apologise for my husband.' There she had a point. 'I am so sorry, I missed that last word you said. I am sorry, did I brush against you there? Sorry, is my head in the way? Sorry, am I in the way? Sorry, I shouldn't really be here. In fact, an empty space would be far better than I.' She brushes trails of hair from her face. 'Sorry I took up this bit of space. I should go, yes? Sorry, I really have to go. Is that rude? I do apologise.' And right before me she made herself as small as air and space would allow till there was barely a handbag on the floor. I looked around to see if anyone was as astonished as I but there were only handbags

and trails of hair where all the women had stood. Their husbands
appeared to be talking to themselves. Maybe this was a common
occurrence. As I bent to examine the bag, a voice beside me said,
'I am sorry, I shouldn't have left it there!' Then even the bag
vanished!

The women in the audience nodded when I read that one.
I think they could hear themselves like I heard myself:

Pale and common
in the docks,
the woman who committed an action.
The judge a red beetroot,
barristers pink puffing stalks.
No one would represent her,
her lawyer was mute
even the crayon nibs of
the newspaper artists
hummed bemusement,
unable to commit her to paper.

At last the judge wheezed out
'Do you have any possible defence you wish to make?'
[I would pause here and run my eye over the audience like
I was that white-wigged man who had decided our fates
for years]
to which she smiled and said,
'I strayed out of the passive tense
looking for something less tame
I think you might have to commit me,
I know I will do it again!'

This time the women laughed. I got intellectual about it, started writing prose – essays, articles, commentary...

> *Women turn into objects as wood petrifies into rock, so silent as to be unnoticed. It takes not thousands of years but only a few in a society that values their aesthetic worth beyond any remnant of humanity.*
>
> *Women can make wonderful pets, excellent door prizes, and pretty good wives as they harden up and gradually feel nothing, no regret even, only the faint pleasure of being so desirable and sought after, fossilised as they are in silk-sealed jars, feet broken backwards and bandaged to make their value soar, metaphorically speaking of course, bandaged feet is not a ritual performed here, though women still have trouble walking upright. Instead they tilt often, incline their heads and nod like dollies with broken springs for necks. It's petrifying to watch a woman and strangely numbing to become one.*

I started questioning the rules. All of them. Why do we have to write in straight lines? Why do we have to be 'rational'? What's so great about poetry as men have made it? It's so Boooooooooring! What about sound? There's so much playing to do with sound. I started screwing around with every convention I knew. Everything I had learned, studied, eaten like it was the holy body of Christ himself. I was having mass reflux:

> *My pump handle action is a plump rump sumptuously bared, scrum diddly umptious, do you have the gumption to play, red pumps ankles suede riddly bumping screwing tongue ump ump ump games?*

Screwing. I was questioning things in that area as well. I mean, I had never *enjoyed* it with men. A lot of women with husbands and boyfriends said they never really *enjoyed* it. Why have women had to lie back and think of 'England'? Why has it been a wife's 'duty'? It's funny how things work, like there was a massive clock tocking in the sky. And at the time I was getting curious, I first saw Sophie.

At the end of one performance night two women came up to me, Angie and Jan. They said they 'loved my work'. I liked them instantly, of course. We went out for a drink, got sloshed on wine and great chatter. Then it was dawn and I found myself spinning into sleep on the floor of their flat. The next morning, they invited me down to Bondi where they were meeting some friends. I borrowed a pair of dark glasses and Angie's jeans. I was sitting on the sand, rolling up the jeans, trying to ignore my stomach pitching up and down with the waves, when I saw her coming out of the water. She wasn't beautiful in a 'Miss Fresher' way. She had thick eyebrows and her long black hair, now wet, clung to her shoulders. Her cheekbones were sharp and she had eyes that ate you up. She looked like a print I had seen in a gallery of Frida Kahlo. She walked straight up to me.

'Are you coming in?' It was more a command. I squinted up at her.

'I don't know. Aren't there sharks at Bondi?' She laughed, flashing a row of small pointed teeth. She stretched out next to me on the sand.

Her shark teeth blink at me. A smile perhaps. She is not letting anything out. I would not play kiss and tell with her.

Or would I?

I got that flying feeling, like when I was on the swings or playing marbles. I wanted to write poetry for her...

She comes out of the sea
all shark teeth and virginity
bursting with buds
of seaweed and crayfish
she unbuttons herself
in my face
lies on the sand
passive and
terribly active

'I see you've met Soph.' Angie came up behind us with the esky of beer. 'You'd better be careful. I think she likes you.'

While she often crossed my mind, I didn't see Sophie again for a month. Jan wanted me to go to Melbourne with her. She had friends there who were getting together a group of women's plays. They were having a performance night at a theatre called La Mama.

'You have to come. They're having trouble finding women's plays. The men have scared them off. Practically all plays produced are written by men. We've got to get a foothold. It's our duty!'

'But I'm not a playwright.'

'That's exactly what they want you to think!'

I was scared shitless but Jan was persuasive. We stayed with Mona, a friend of hers. She had divorced her husband after being freed from servitude by the women's movement or, as she put it *The Female Eunuch*. Now she was a single mum stuck with three kids.

The house was crazy. This was the place I was meant to write my first play! Every time I found a quiet corner and got down to writing, one of the brats would sniff me out then all of them would descend – Indians, cowboys, vegemite fingers, sticky faces over my paper. But they weren't my kids, so I smiled and sat on my hands so I wouldn't whack them. I spared a thought for all the mums who tried to write and the dads who got to lock themselves away 'cause they were 'professional', and had wives to keep the hordes at bay. What I'd give for a wife! All I ended up writing was this little poem.

What is an interruption?

A plague on the cream of your crop
A page left blank
Amnesia in an instant
The light switched off

The empty room
marked only by the swing of a door
latch shut –
frustration swells
like a bruise,
a mute interrogation
What was there before this space?

And if you could kill the source,
the innocents tugging at your skirts
the lady selling her jam
swipe them dead as a fly
you would.

Medea
contemplating devastation
on the brink of a tea cup
pen brush frozen
even as it falls
dumb hand
suspended
sinking
where before there were oceans
lit with sails.

…But no play.

In the end, the play came from talking to Mona. Over cups of tea, she told me about the hesitation, the doubt, the moments of clarity that pre-empted her divorce. I came up with a one-act play called *An Act of Will*. There I was dressed as a housewife in Mona's apron and stockings in front of rows of women squashed in a space the size of a walk-in wardrobe. La Mama's foyer was a brick courtyard taken up by a dunny. Women poured in from Lygon Street, sipping their wine in paper cups and stamping their feet to keep out the Melbourne cold. I was the opening act. I was shaking as I sat on the couch. It was pretty dark. There was a spotlight but it was over to the side, not on me. I said something like this.

'I'm re-con-dit-ioning myself, you know, like a motor or a washing machine or a fridge. I figure it might take some time. You don't mind waiting, do you? Are you sure that's okay? I wouldn't want to put you out?' (I say it all in this wheedling voice.)

'Would you like a cuppa tea? Cake? Milk...? Oh look, I'm doing it again. I've got to shut up. Every time I open my mouth, out it comes. That old shit. I'm done with that. I'm done with it, I tell you. I'm getting re-con-dit-ioned.' (I drag out that word, say it like it's a new big word for me.)

'I'm...how do they say it? Raising my conscience...no, no...raising my consciousness.' (So I just sit there a bit, let the time tick on. Then I start whistling and getting bored. I wait till the audience is shuffling around in their seats.)

'It's taking a while, isn't it? Maybe I should put this spotlight on me. That'd help. That'll do the trick. Hey you!' (I wave my arm at the spotlight.)

'Over here!' (The spotlight doesn't budge. I get up and try and stand under it. It keeps dodging me. I start chasing it around.)

'You bloody well come 'ere. Don't tell me I'm nagging. Don't tell me I'm hysterical. You come here right this minute. Wait till your father comes home!' (When I say this last bit, the spotlight stops abruptly. I climb into it.)

'There, you see. I can do this.' (Then I start puffing myself up a bit, standing taller.)

'I deserve this. I deserve this.' (I say it soft and get louder.)

'I am worth it. I am a real person. I matter. I do exist.' (I get excited and start jumping around.)

'Hey, look at me! Look at me! I'm terrific, I'm terrific!' (And go on like that for a bit until I get tired. Then I stop as if examining something.)

'No, no good. Still feel like shit. All right, you bastards.' (I get out some dolls from a kid's toy box in the corner. I hold up Flash Gordon. Start kicking him around.)

'There, see, how do you like it? I'm as good as you. I'm every inch as good as you!' (I get mad, rip off the apron.)

'Fuck, fuck, fuck, fuck fuck, vag-in-a, vag-in-a. I'll get you a bloody cup of tea!' (There's a table with a china tea set laid out on it behind the couch. I go over, splatter the milk around, pour it all over myself and start smashing the tea cups, tearing off my clothes.)

'Don't say I'm hysterical. You'd be hysterical too!' (As I'm going crazy, the husband walks in. This is Jan in drag, 'cause we had a no-man policy for the show. Not that they were beating our door down to be in it! The minute he/she enters, the spotlight goes right on him.)

'Hi, darling, I'm home. What's for dinner?' (Husband doesn't even look at me, doesn't blink an eyelid, despite the fact I'm covered in milk and half-naked now. He sits at the table and gets out the newspaper.)

'Oh, love, you're home. Would you like a cuppa tea? (I go pick up pieces of the broken china cups. Then stop and sit on the couch. I look at the audience and sigh.)

'Takes a bit to get re-con-dit-ioned, doesn't it?'

Curtain drops. Or it would if there had been a curtain. As it was the spotlight just blacked out. Applause. Jan and I gave a bow. Laughter as she whips off her fake beard and takes the banana out of her pants.

A lot of fun that night. After the plays, a huge group of us went out and terrorised the local pubs. We got one review from a man who hadn't even seen it. He tried to make a joke of us, saying we were a bitter and twisted lot who had got ourselves all worked up and just needed a good fuck. The old frigid bitches line. But he was right about one thing.

When I got back to Sydney, I found a message from Soph, inviting me over for dinner to celebrate my 'stardom'.

She's cooking curry. We open a bottle of wine and the talk flows smooth as the booze down my throat. She is a sculptor, acrobat and dancer, all between working in a women's refuge. She asks me what I want my life to be. All I can think of to say is that I like to write, yeah, I want to be a writer.

'What the hell you doing studying teaching then?' She tilts her glass up to drain the last drop.

As if it were that easy, that clear-cut. Just go and have what you want. Life is a feast! Her thoughts are strung in ways I would never imagine myself. She sees colours as if they were frozen in time. She wipes her hands on the orange towel while the curry boils in the background.

I think I am in love. We never get around to the curry that night.

Her lips expand
a doorframe in the heat
all oxygen and ocean
I lay my tongue
a wet dog at that door
currying favours
currying crumbs…

Her liquor rises
stronger than acid
burning my thumbs
as I pull her apart
I arch my fingers

across her arse
deep into her muscles
now they pull me apart

And I am careening like a
wild western cowgirl
driving fast off a
yellow brick road
her cunt is bigger than
a Lover's Moon
I am Jonah
she swallows me whole

The next day, my body buzzing, my head rattling and the taste of Soph sweet on my tongue, I go to uni and change over to Arts. I'm going to be a writer. The art of taking yourself seriously when no one else does requires a certain vision over the tripping wires of your own self-doubt. I go out to celebrate and drown my fears with Jan. She told me to beware the 'angel in the house'. I thought the grog had got to her but she told me it was from Virginia Woolf, who urged women to kill the angel in the house, the 'good woman' they had been moulded into by men. I started thinking about the voices that went on in my head when I wrote. It was bloody noisy. There was a crowd of wagging fingers, raised eyebrows, stern nods...

Am I a fly in the ink now?
Watching squeezed emotions
fly through the pen
no good

not bad
quite effective
maybe I judge all the time
a silent critic
loud in your head
the fly in the ink
comparing talents with the fly on the wall.

I told Jan I would get rid of the angel and all her devils. She wished me luck and we decided it was a mission worth toasting, so we ordered another round. That night I stumbled up to Soph's flat.

'Your arse is the shape of the glass I sip, round and whisky full,' I slurred as she opened the door.

She wrapped her arms around me. She was wearing a red dressing gown, sleeping eyes barely open.

'Anon, my horny poetess. Come to bed.'

We had barely spent a night apart since that first time. The moonlight filtered through the tie-dyed curtain she's hung above her bed. It stained the walls with orange and blue shadows. The colours swam across her face as she slept.

Love is gentle and scary.

…I want you
so tight
you can never
go or be taken
as nothing moves or changes
not a hair
just breath and love
I cave in

at any kink of absence
it hurts,
you wriggle away
I am demanding
I need to stop time

The year lurched on in a tumble of love, sex, study and writing. I tried to learn the ropes of every game. They were slippery. I did my end-of-year paper on women, despite my lecturer telling me I'd never have a serious academic career if I kept going down that track. I called it, 'Loaded women: our literary sisterhood.'

I was excited about it, even looking forward to presenting it to my fellow students and teachers. Despite all my work with women's lib, it had not occurred to me there could be a full-scale attack rallying around my paper. At my presentation, I found myself surrounded by jaded bastions of the unfairer sex. I felt like a newly minted coin compared to them. Their egos were the most vital part of their anatomy. Everything else was dust and fear. It was so fragile, one kick and the whole structure had a stake to lose. Maybe it's harder for men to come down from their perches than it is for us women to climb. The hardest part, after all, of being king is staying king.

The men screeched first, came up to me first and left first. The women held back, boiling with opinions, but they would not take the space and, with these men, it would not be given. They spoke last, approached me last and stayed to buzz around me like bees. As I had managed to return fire, I was the queen bee of the moment. I had dared to stir the hornets' nest. The hornets themselves had shown their sting, and we celebrated after with champagne just how little poison their tiny pricks held. This, however, we already knew. As I sipped my drink and made dark jokes about the faculty as a mausoleum for dead white men, I wondered what it would take for these women to show their own precious bite.

As for me, my own muzzle was still intact, the joints oiled to my jaw. While the hinges were hanging loose, I never bit, never broke entirely free from the contraption, fused as it was to my body at birth. That training as a girl that made stroking men's egos an instinct, feeding, fellating the monsters…Thank you, Sir, thank you, Sir…I appreciate that criticism…At times, the anger worked like a fuel. I would be that swashbuckling heroine I had searched for as a child. I would grind them all down…

> …*My tongue*
> *wrecks you.*
> *Is it that it*
> *leaves you unhung*
>   *or*
> *like a woman*
> *in a Greek tragedy,*
> *no tongue*
> *to incriminate?*
> *No hands to write my name?*
>
> *Is that what*
> *keeps you up this icy night?*
> *My tongue in*
> *your ears,*

lisping recriminations,
bathing your cheeks
in spit?

Other times, it left me as good as dead. When I tried to write, it would get noisy and hard. I would bail, get pissed and stoned with Angie and Jan.

> *…Would I write something now if the expectation of failure didn't stick like the gall of failing to cum? I am so tired of wrestling with my angel and her ghosts. I shudder in the glow of wanting to show and of big fear.*

I'd get so down after the grog and grass. My past lay in wait, ready to float fragments of memory to the surface. Me in my red bathers, a starfish on the rocks, my dad rolling home drunk…

> *The girl by the well is strung into plucked wire. The sound of water is crazy that far down. The stones drop and echo ways out. She stretches her wrists and shows sad melodramatic lines, tight and red as her lips all puckered up for kisses. And to ask her to take it out instead of in is like asking a one-way road to turn backward, a loop of tar u-turning to face its own white line. Lines now all strung tight as a guitar, her lips, wrists, the black tar of the road, the white line, I level up my anger with my own spiteful arrow, aim it down the well and miss. I shoot myself in the foot.*

Dragging my way through this old hatbox is like cleaning the gutters or the gully trap. When I dig through these crumpled papers, read them all together, it kinda makes sense how I got here. It's not hard to see why Soph stopped coming around. And when I went there after a late night, I'd knock and knock and the lights stayed off. I felt like my dad rocking on my feet on her welcome mat. When we did see each other, she was harsh to me, cruel. I wondered where the soft Soph went. She'd go on and on about the drink and dope. Biting words left me flat as roadkill:

> *All your tiny bullets*
> *are mounted*
> *on the headrest to your bed.*
> *I watch you lay waste,*
> *every time you speak*
> *someone's shot down,*
> *mostly me.*

I couldn't see how dark I was. I was spinning in my own cyclone, Cyclone Susie. Yep, she left a path of destruction. Nothing standing after she came through town. When Soph finally said the words, I was shattered. I played Bob Dyl, curled up in a ball to 'It's All Over Now, Baby Blue'. I went through six packs of cigarettes in one night. Funny, when things come apart you can't say how or when it started exactly, like one thread gets loose you hadn't noticed and you're left with knots and holes. All I saw was holes and I was falling down each one of them.

The thing about falling is you either stay down or get up. There are no two ways. And there's comfort in hitting the bottom, knowing what it looks like down that well. Something scary about not knowing disappears. You test your strength and feel it as you crawl out. I suppose that's what I'm doing here. You trawl through your life when you're putting it together after a cyclone's hit. Like I said, I don't have photos.

Every moment is a pulse on the clock
Demanding a performance, right word, right strategy, steer left,
now write, in, out, wheedle, steer clear

Come on strong with your mighty chains of silver tongue

Make it clear you come studied, accessories at hand

You come with metal lashes, a studded strap to belt the dogs down

And when it is quiet, you stand in empty space, breathe a while,
the scent of words to say, reasons, declarations, war, knees, feet,
paws, claws, at the ready, at
command

And when the trees creak underfoot, muscles jump

Attack

And armies of old men with fear for bones lie at your feet

Then close your eyes again, feel compassion even

Sway in the moment
Everything is on your ground, at your feet, the oyster, the world,
the whole of
your armour resting soft against you.

The Last Word

The floor is hard as I sit, crossed-legged on the rug. I hadn't sat this way since I was in kindergarten. The sound of Susie's voice has a rhythm to it like a swing. Everything on my ground...at my feet...The whole of my armour resting soft against me. I become aware of my skin as it folds over my body. I feel something, a strength I pull up from inside me. At first it is only like a string, then it becomes thicker like rope and then I have reams of it, weaving itself into chain mail. It travels over my chest, my knees, my throat, my back until I am completely encased in a silver sheath of armour. It is the softest metal I have ever seen. It feels more like silk, and the links that weave it together are fine and delicate. They slot into each other so there is not a single gap. They fit like the feathers of a bird or the scales of a snake.

When I look up, Susanne has gone. The hatbox has disappeared. There is no sign that she was ever here except for the curl of smoke from her last cigarette. It lies gutted in the fireplace. Sybylla takes in my new attire.

'It suits you,' she says. 'You look impenetrable.'

And I did. I felt in that moment as if nothing could touch me.

'What is it made of?' I ask.

Sybylla stands up and goes over to the open window. A cool breeze lifts her hair from her shoulders. 'You don't need to ask me questions any more. You know the answers. Our journey is coming to an end.'

I do know it. It is not only the progression of time. It is a feeling. Through the open window I hear a church bell toll. I could be anywhere in any time. That sound has existed for centuries…The bell, the raven, the kingfisher, the snake, the egg, the feather; what drifts lightly falls hard.

'Take a look around this room.' Sybylla rests back on the window frame. 'Does any of this look familiar?'

I look around properly for the first time. Before I had been distracted by Susanne and her hatbox. Now it is empty and in the morning light I can see more clearly the outline of the room, the cobwebs in the corners, the dust on the mantelpiece. It is very old and there are metal rings in the walls. It is as if it were once a gymnasium or a nursery. There has been much activity here, as the floorboards are gouged and splintered. I notice then that the walls were once covered in wallpaper. It has faded almost to white but I can still make out the yellow stain. There is not much left on the wall. Strips of it have been torn off the whole way around the room. It looks like someone has been frantic in getting it off. Half the wallpaper looks chewed and the other half is scraped as if by frenzied nails. I look at Sybylla.

'This place needs a renovation.'

She laughs.

'It most certainly does.'

'You could go mad getting all that stuff off.'

'Yes. It has been known to happen.'

I follow the stripped paper with my eye. There is a streak that runs around the bottom of it. It is a smudge of yellow that continues all the way around the room just inches from the skirting board. If one were to creep along the wall, it is exactly where the shoulder would fit. It occurs to me that, to be seeing the yellow wallpaper, we must no longer be inside the pattern. We must have got out. I remember Sybylla saying, once we had entered the wallpaper, the only way out was to peel it off strip by strip, story by story.

'*We have to meet the women who are caught under it or there is no way for them to get out. Or us. That's what happens when you enter a story. You become it. They are not safe things, stories. They are not for bedtime with a hot cup of milk, like you've been told. They're dangerous. Don't forget you almost drowned...*'

The journey has been hazardous to say the least. I hope they are out, those women – Lucy, Vera, Stella, Ruby, Eve... Susie. I hope they feel the fresh air on their skin and breathe in their freedom.

'Come to the window,' Sybylla says. 'There is quite a view.'

The view is breathtaking. There is a garden with grass so green you want to drink it. It is large and shady with pathways all through it paved with sandstone. The paths are lined with long grape-covered arbours. There are seats underneath the arbours perfect for sitting in and reading. It is hard to see where the paths lead. They run off into bushes. They are hidden behind trees. These green corridors travel to secret places, secret gardens with gates and locks, rivers and lakes, even fountains. As I look closer I notice movement on the paths. There is someone down there. I lean out the window and squint. A woman is sitting on a seat under one of the arbours, writing in a book.

Have you ever looked at the ground and it all seems so still and bare, then after you have been looking a few moments you see one ant then two until you realise the whole ground is crawling with them? The earth beneath your feet has been alive with creatures the entire time. This is the sensation I have now. I see one woman, then another walking in the shadows beneath the blackberry vines, and another and another. The entire garden is teeming with women. They all look at home, as if they belong here. They are not creeping about. They are drawing, playing, running. Some are simply lying on the grass. I lean out the window a little more and I can hear laughter now, and the sounds of chatter. I even think I hear singing...yes, there is that song... Someone is singing.

'*Fly high, Birdie, fly high. To the sky. To the sky. Birdie, Birdie, gonna fly high. Gonna fly high, to the sky.*'

I turn as I realise it is Sybylla. She smiles at me and laughs a gleeful laugh that splits her face into a sun and the light is so bright I have to shield my eyes.

'Don't worry,' she says, stroking the silver metal of my skin. 'You are impenetrable now. You won't break any bones. Remember us. Write us a story sometime.'

She leans towards me and places a kiss on my lips. It is the softest shiver of a touch. Warm and cold as if it were laced with vodka and ice. I feel her hand on my back as she pushes me out the window ledge. I am drowning. I am falling...

I think that woman goes out in the daytime!
And I'll tell you why – privately – I've seen her!
I can see her out of every one of my windows!

they suddenly commit suicide – plunge off at outrageous angles,
destroy themselves in unheard of contradictions…

and I'd sell my soul for total control…

…Do people make their life easier by saying that over and over
like worn beads on a rosary?

I'm all broken up over you…

How fast the fall from visionary to monkey and all in the glide of
the slippery slide between one's legs…
crack in time to the splintering of my whalebone heart

another cup of tea…

…And would she notice
if I am the pin that bursts her bubble?

would you like a little bonfire for breakfast?

…Fly, fly, Birdie, fly…

…I am demanding
I need to stop time.

The faces swim in glass, cloudy as a dream. I see the crowd of women through my glass of water. The liquid distorts their shapes. I adjust my vision. Now they are sitting straight again like blades of grass. In front of me, my page looks harmless, covered in inky scrawling. What looked like goblins and blackberry vines are only marks on paper. The rivers are ink blots that have leaked over the edges. Sybylla is still there. I see the shape of her head and her long blackberry skirt but she is frozen. Her eyes are closed. She does not move. She does not speak. She is a figure I drew. The touch of her lips is distant, a nerve sensation from another time. A memory.

Onstage, the woman I sketched onto my paper, Sybil Jones, is still talking. I cannot see right through her any more. She is solid, her cinnamon hair down to her shoulders, her hands trembling a little as she turns the pages of her book. Either side of me, heads are nodding in serious contemplation of the speaker. No one in the audience is looking at me queerly. I wonder if perhaps I am still invisible when I catch the eye of the woman with the stiff spine. She is the one who started all this mess with her sneaking into the chintz pattern of her curtain and making blood pacts with wolves, the one who started me wondering what lay behind the eyes of these women watching us now with such diligence.

Wondering turns to wandering and that is where the danger begins.

No hot cup of milk before bedtime indeed.

The woman notices my eyes on her. She meets them and sends a smile over the heads of the women in the front row.

Everything seems in place. Everything is as it was. But it is not.

My armour rests against my body like skin.

'*"I've got out at last" said I "in spite of you…I've pulled off most of the paper so you can't put me back"*. And that was the truth. That was, one could say, her last word.'

Onstage, Sybil Jones closes the story of *The Yellow Wallpaper*. The clapping of the audience is no polite clatter of hands. The women are glowing, as if she has spoken straight to them. Sybil blushes, her cheeks turning a faint rose beneath her brown skin.

'Thank you,' she takes a last sip of her water and sits back down behind the table.

A balding man takes her place at the lectern to instruct us that book signings will commence shortly and to make our way to the foyer for tea and coffee. A crowd of women instantly gathers around Ms Jones. I head into the foyer. A lady rushes to fetch me a cup of coffee. I thank her. I could certainly do with a coffee. I am not up for chatter now. I see an alcove with a chair near the banister. I try to make my way to it before anyone can seize me. As I move forward, I hit an elbow and almost go skidding over the carpet. Coffee splashes on my shirt and the cuff of my sleeve.

'Sorry, sorry…' I turn to see a woman apologising as much as I am. 'Sorry, sorry.'

Her coffee has splashed over her as well. I see stains on her red skirt. Looking down there are the Jarrah heels and chocolate stockings. As I look up, she laughs, 'We must really stop apologising.'

Her eyes are not murky like a pond at all. They are clear as glass marbles. I do not know what to say now she is in front of me. If I say her speech changed my life or even mention Sybylla, I will sound crazy.

'I hadn't read *The Yellow Wallpaper* before,' I say. 'It sounds hypnotic the way Gilman talks about all those patterns.'

'That story changed my life,' Sybil Jones looks at me for a moment, and then smiles. Her smile is like Sybylla's when she creeps into my thoughts. 'Some stories are dangerous, aren't they?'

I stare at her, remembering the feel of Sybylla's lips on mine. 'Yes, I could see that.'

We stand in the midst of the crowd. People mill around us, drinking, laughing, locked in conversation. Eventually the bald man comes and tells us it is time to sign the books. Queues of woman are lined up for signatures. I begin to apologise a final time, when Sybil stops me.

'I don't believe anything is by chance, do you?' She smiles back over her shoulder as she walks to the desk allotted to her. I see her whisper something to each woman who comes up for an autograph. They grin and start to shine a little more. It is as if they are matches. One by one she lights them up.

I sit at my desk. As the women come up to me with my latest book to be signed I look at them differently. I study their faces, not as if they were a procession of similar types, boxed and labelled. I look beyond that to each line, each crack, each mannerism. The way one constantly puts her hand up to her lips as if scared of saying the wrong thing reminds me of Stella. The strut of another takes me back to Vera. One who looks immaculate, not a hair out of place, could be Eve. Who knows what any of us may be, in any time?

The book they hand me seems to be written by a stranger. It is called *Improbable Lies* and has gold lettering embossed on the cover of the book. Did I have any idea what to say before now? Did I see anyone properly? Or do you feel like this every time you expand a little? Everything I knew in the past appears so narrow in retrospect, like looking down a hallway, merging to one definitive point. Everything ahead is open. Nothing is certain.

That evening when I come home, I race to see Byron. I feel like I have been away from her for a century. And I have. I hold her close. The babysitter is telling me to let her breathe.

'Yes, yes,' I say. Of course she must breathe.

Her skin…soft…Not a crease on it yet. I rest her against my shoulder as she wakes up. There is nothing like seeing a baby wake up. It is like watching the dawn, only more intimate. The babysitter is gone now and the house is still, just the two of us alone. She is easy to dress in her sleepy state. I put a singlet, a jumper, a jacket on her and then place her on my hip. I walk with her like this down to the park. The swings are empty. There is no one around. It is too late for children to come out now. No one is having barbecues at dusk.

I sit for a while beneath a great old elm. Its leaves tower in a massive umbrella. It is coming around to autumn, and a few of them are leaving their branches early. They flutter down at random to light upon the earth. Like gold rain, Eve said. I follow the massive roots down into the ground, imagining them sucking up the water in the soil. So thirsty – that was Vera: thirsty and never enough to drink. But there is something comforting about the roots now. Byron is getting restless. She is tossing in my arms. I walk over to the swings and put her on my lap as I rock us back and forth. I can't help myself. I start humming Sybylla's song.

'*Fly high, Birdie, fly high. To the sky. To the sky. You're gonna fly.*'

And as I hum, I can hear her. She is behind me whispering over my shoulder as she pushes the swing ever so gently.

'We will lie between the worlds, you and I, pressed here against the letters and the page, caressed perhaps by a hand in passing, a rare touch that moves us for years. Here we will watch and walk, wait and let the faces wander by, a thought here, a catch of an eye threads a needle through a hook… all the weavers silent and dead, all the ones talking still, all those tossing restless in their nest, the itch of ink hissing now in midget fingers, fists balled small as mandarins. Can you see this one's fists, heavy with juice?'

I look down at Byron. She is playing with the gold chain around my neck. Her hands curl and uncurl as she tries to fasten on to the slippery metal.

'Can you see her story crawling now as she crawls between spaces whiter than her new teeth? Her tongue sticks out between her lips, testing the pitch of the wind. It will start to sing soon, a tuning fork struck in the stillness. Its red tip will hum like the point of a water diviner smelling rivers beneath the earth. It is then her fists unravel and her fingers wriggle. See,' says Sybylla, 'they are ink-stained already. They have a lot on their minds.'

Byron's hands are not stained with ink. They have a spot of orange paint on them, that is all. But who knows what Sybylla sees? I do not doubt her. That night as I wrap Byron up in her blankets, I begin to tell her a story. It is one that will take a long time to finish and I have to admit that even I do not know the ending. But I like the beginning, and for now that is all we need.

'Every so often, in one moment of a day, it falls on a person to do one small thing that changes the course of that day for many people. This is one of those days…'

Acknowledgements

I would like to express my thanks to the judges of the Dorothy Hewett Award and to UWA Publishing, Terri-ann White, Charlotte Guest, Kate Pickard, Alissa Dinallo and all the staff, for helping with the editing and development of this manuscript.

Drawing Sybylla is a story which emerged from my PhD study, researching the past and conversations with women in the present about courage, suppression and creative freedom. As I began to dig, I realised how many women were missing from the curriculum I was taught. To hear their voices across time was sometimes tough, sad, shocking but always illuminating, passionate and inspiring – just a few of the names I wish I had know better growing up and in my literature degree...Miles Franklin, Barbara Baynton, Eleanor Dark, Marjorie Barnard, Flora Eldershaw, Nettie Palmer, Katharine Susannah Prichard, Christina Stead, Charmian Clift, Dorothy Hewett, Ruby Langford Ginibi, Oodgeroo Noonuccal (Kath Walker), Judith Wright, Jean Devanny, Barbara Hanrahan, all the fighters for women's rights...and so many more...I was treated with amazing generosity of time and wisdom by the women who agreed to speak with me and share experiences of their writing life.

Thanks to Dr Christine Ferrari for supervising and advising me through those years.

Thanks to the School of Culture and Communication and my talented colleagues in Creative Writing at the University of Melbourne whose welcome sparked the pulling of this story from its own proverbial dusty drawer.

Endless gratitude to the people closest who kept me literally fed in body and heart. My sister – my rock. Chrissy Davidson and her lovely mum Barbara; Rachel Forgasz; Nathan Parker; and friends who listened, read and shared this with me. Dianne Jones, who lived with the noisy women from this story invisible but so loud in our hallway, thanks for your creativity, spirit and belief. My Kelada family – Gillian, Boulos, Helena, Alex – words are useless for capturing so many years of love, keeping me grounded and make it worth it.

And to the women I came from over generations, centuries and seas whose stories I would love to be able to hear.